CW00746735

CROW

AMBER R. DUELL & CANDACE ROBINSON

Midnight Tide
PUBLISHING

FOR TRACY

CHAPTER ONE

CROW

TWENTY-ONE YEARS AGO

Life was full of beautiful moments, though few as precious as the birth of a daughter.

Crow had known when Reva told him she was pregnant that his life would be permanently brighter. The small, wrinkled baby on Reva's chest had taken a single breath and, with it, his soul.

"What name do you think fits her?" Reva asked in a tired voice.

Crow shifted closer on the large, four-post bed and wrapped his arm around the love of his life. Sweat coated her face, her brown hair clinging to her forehead, but she had never looked more beautiful. His gaze drifted from the baby to Reva's emerald eyes and back again.

"We'll know it when it comes to us," Crow replied, placing a kiss on her temple. They hadn't spoken of names before—they couldn't without seeing the child. True names needed to fit the individual, and he was too overcome with the new, euphoric love

1

to think clearly enough for such an important task.

The baby cooed and Reva lifted the child from her chest to stare thoughtfully at her. Crow took in their daughter's gently pointed ears, identical to Reva's, and the chin that resembled his own. She also had his brown eyes, though her hair was too sparse to know if it was as dark as his or brown like Reva's. Their child seemed to have inherited the best of them both—not that Crow was biased.

"You have no suggestions?" Reva arched a brow and tilted her head.

When Crow took the baby's hand, her fingers wrapped tightly around his thumb. A name began to take shape in the back of his mind, still too vague to make out. When the time was right, they would *know*. All parents did. "I once knew a tree spirit named Gurbera," he offered playfully.

"Absolutely not!" Reva hugged the child to her chest and laughed. Then cringed. "Ow."

"Let me hold her," Crow said quickly. "You've labored for nearly a day. You should rest."

Reva sighed and snuggled closer into Crow's side. "I am rather tired."

"Sleep, my love. I'll have Whispa prepare something for you to eat when you wake."

"Let her rest too." Reva yawned. "She was up with me the entire time."

The pixie had been a lifesaver. Crow had no idea how to help with the delivery of a child. Fae children were so rare—he'd never even seen one so young before this day, let alone witnessed the miracle firsthand. But Whispa had seen Reva's family through multiple generations.

"Of course." Crow kissed Reva's lips quickly and slid from the bed while cradling their sleeping daughter. She was so small. So perfect. "Leave everything to me."

Reva offered a faint smile, her eyes already fluttering shut. His fierce, beautiful, powerful Reva. She appeared exhausted, but

2

content. The labor hadn't been an easy one and it had taken almost every ounce of Reva's energy to see it through. When she woke, she would be ravenous. Making a warm meal was the absolute least he could do.

Crow laid his daughter down beside Reva instead of putting her into the bassinet. The smooth wooden basket hung from thick vines attached to the ceiling so it could gently rock, and the firm pillow inside was covered in the softest of furs. Reva and Whispa had spent a week weaving strands of delicate, enchanted wild flowers through the latticework. But Crow didn't want to leave such a tiny child so far across the room. Pausing in the doorway for a lingering look, Crow watched Reva pull their baby closer and shut her eyes. He left for the kitchen, feeling he might explode from joy.

"Oh!" Whispa gasped when they nearly collided on the staircase. Smoky gray hair skimmed her jawline and the first hint of fine lines showed near her honey-colored eyes. The red and blue patterned dress she wore was rumpled and stained after the delivery, and her thin, glimmering wings drooped with fatigue. "Is everything well with Lady Reva and the child?"

"Everything is wonderful." Crow lifted the four-foot pixie into a hug, and she squealed as he swung her in a circle. When he set her back down, she was blushing all the way to the tips of her ears. "They're both asleep. You should rest too."

She pursed her lips as if weighing the suggestion. "After I check on the lady, perhaps."

"You're too hard-working, Whispa." Crow smiled warmly and continued down the stone stairs. He glanced back before he lost sight of her and, in a serious voice, added, "You have to take care of yourself."

Whispa's good-natured *tsk* reached his ears as he continued his descent, followed immediately by the sound of glass exploding. Crow froze mid-step. "Whispa?" he called, hoping the pixie simply broke a vase.

But he knew she hadn't. The crash was far too loud for that.

3

He bolted back to the second floor and skidded to a halt the moment he hit the landing. Whispa writhed on the floor among thousands of tiny glass shards, the large circular window at the end of the hall demolished. Her thin, crystalline wings were in tatters and blood spilled down her arms and legs from the cuts.

Crow's boots crunched on the glass, the sound echoing. "Whispa! What happened?" There were no trees near the house that could've caused this, and the weather was calm.

"Lady... Reva..." she croaked, curling into a fetal position.

Crow's world slowed as his gaze shifted from the pixie to the open bedroom door. *No, no, no, no, no!*

"Leave!" Reva roared from the bedroom.

A cold, feminine chuckle sounded in response, chilling the blood in his veins. Not *her.* Anyone but her... Stomach churning, Crow burst into the room he had vacated moments ago to find Reva shielding their child in her arms. The *Good* Witch of the North, Locasta, stood at the foot of the bed. Crow knew from experience that Locasta was as wicked as they came. He'd tried to leave her so many times after he'd realized *good* had nothing to do with the witch. She'd given out food to her people when they were hungry, but only enough to keep them from rioting. Offered cures that contained scant amounts of poison to fix the overpopulation. Fae that defied her were secreted away to be killed—some immediately, some after torture—but the Northern Witch assured the families that her guards were searching for their lost loved ones. She had frequently gone so far as to create *proof* of her efforts, or sentenced innocents to death for the crimes *she'd* committed.

Locasta had never accepted Crow leaving her though. The abuse had finally become so terrible that he'd fled to the West in search of help to stop Locasta. He'd found none before Reva. And now she stood in the home Crow shared with Reva on the night their child was born. That was too much of a coincidence to believe.

"Locasta," he barked, half in anger, half in fear. His daughter screeched in response. Hadn't they gone deep enough into hiding? How far did Crow need to take his family for them to be safe? "What are you doing here?"

"Ah, there you are, sweetheart." Locasta turned with a dramatic swoosh of her ruby dress. Obsidian hair shone all the way to her narrow waist and eyes, the lightest blue, pierced him. Her full lips quirked into an angry smile. "It's been too long."

Reva clutched the howling baby protectively to her chest with one hand and curled the other into a fist. Green sparks fizzled from between her clenched fingers, her energy too depleted from labor to conjure anything more. "Get her out of here, Crow. Now!"

If he had his choice, Locasta wouldn't only be out of their home, but banished from Oz completely. Unfortunately, she still had her claws in too many influential fae who believed her wicked lies. It would be nearly impossible to exile her through the proper channels. Forcing someone as deranged as Locasta to leave would only stoke the fire anyway, and his family was far too precious to risk her wrath. The situation was already dangerous enough.

"Locasta," Crow said gently, his hands outstretched. "Come with me."

His ex-lover laughed. "I've tried to get *you* to come with *me* for over a year now."

"I know." Crow swallowed hard and forced himself not to look away from her icy glare. She'd found him almost everywhere he and Reva went, sending him either letters proclaiming love, or threats accompanied by bloody appendages of random fae. "We can go downstairs and talk about—"

"The time for talking is over," Locasta seethed, her fists tightening. "You've offended me for the last time, hiding yourself away and breeding with this whore."

A wisp of green smoke streaked through the air toward Locasta, but she avoided it with a quick spin on her heels. It dissipated a moment later. Crow winced at his beloved's attempt to channel her power—that small, harmless bit had to cost her everything she had left.

"Reva, don't," he begged. She was too weak to battle Locasta right now, and his ability to transform into a crow wouldn't do much against the Northern Witch's magic. The best way out of this was to talk Locasta down. He would promise anything to get her to leave, even if it meant going with her. He'd escaped the North once and he could do it again if it meant protecting Reva and their baby.

Reva's eyes narrowed in his direction. She knew Locasta was unhinged—she knew *everything* Crow had suffered while he'd lived in her palace. He'd seen fae tortured on Locasta's orders, and endured the Northern Witch's rage multiple times. His feathers had been plucked, his blood drained until he was dizzy, and, whenever Locasta broke his skin, he'd been forced to take saltwater baths. Each punishment only ended when he was *sufficiently* injured. Sometimes not even then, because she would use her power to force him into his bird form and lock him in a cage. So why did it seem like Reva was angry at *him* for trying to protect her and their daughter? It wasn't possible that she thought he was standing up for his former lover, was it?

"This ends now," Locasta announced. Blue light filled the room and a shriek came from the hallway. *Whispa.*

"Stop." Crow tried to step toward Locasta, but his feet refused to move. The planked floor had transformed around them, shackling him in place. The wood slowly circled higher and higher, past his ankles and around his legs, digging into his flesh. He bent, trying to pry it away, but it was no use. "Locasta, *stop!* Release me."

"Crow!" Reva's desperate cry tore through his chest. When he saw the reason for her outburst, his heart nearly stopped. The bedsheets bound Reva's limbs, strapping her down, and the child... *Oh Gods...* Locasta held her with one arm, blue magic flowing endlessly from the witch's free hand.

"Pixie," Locasta called, chin held high, a victorious smirk on

6

her lips.

Whispa lumbered into the bedroom then, only she wasn't a pixie any longer. Her willowy body seemed to have shrunk—now skeletal with thick, rubbery skin clinging to the bones. Jagged teeth protruded from tightly stretched lips, giving the illusion of a deranged smile, and her eyes had gone completely black. The worst part, however, was the change in her wings from beautiful, crystalline to black leather that hung in uneven pieces from a boney protrusion on her back.

Fear ripped through Crow—not for himself, but for the females around him. Locasta's power to transform anything had always unnerved him, but to see something so gruesome... She had never done anything so drastic before, and that terrified him most of all. The *Good* Witch seemed to have finally lost her senses completely.

"Locasta, please," Crow begged. "Stop this. Don't hurt them, and I'll go to the North with you, I swear. Just *please* don't hurt them." He would sacrifice himself for Reva and their child. Every. Single. Time.

"I begged you not to hurt *me* too," she said, spittle flying in his direction. "You"—she addressed the beast that was Whispa and held the baby out—"fly this *thing* North. Stop for nothing and no one. Wait for me in the highest tower and do not let it die."

"You stupid bitch!" Reva screamed. "If you dare take my daughter, I swear you will die a slow, painful death at my hands."

Crow struggled harder against the wood, now encasing his waist. Locasta couldn't take their baby. She *couldn't*. He had to stop this now before she handed her to the beastly pixie.

"Shut your filthy mouth," Locasta spat.

Whispa took the child, pulled her close, and darted out the broken window before Crow could even free a single splinter.

"No!" Crow and Reva cried in unison.

Crow fought against Locasta's magic with every ounce of strength he had. If he transformed into his bird form, Locasta's

7

magic would snap him up and hold him tighter—he'd tried flying away from her temper before. But that was his daughter. *His daughter!* His heart shattered inside his chest.

"I will slaughter you for this," Reva spat, tears sliding down her cheeks.

"For your sake," Locasta said to Crow, "she'll become a changeling instead of a corpse."

"Give her back to me!" Reva's hands flexed and curled, unable to create a single spark. "Give her *back!*"

The floor wove up to Crow's midsection, stopping just below his heart. "Take me, Locasta. Please."

"We aren't finished yet." With a swirl of her hands, Locasta sent her magic blasting into Reva's chest.

Reva screamed until her voice was raw, and Crow shouted along with her as Locasta's magic faded from the air. The sheets released their grip on Reva and she rolled, falling to the floor, unconscious—or nearly so. Her eyes rolled beneath their lids, and her neck muscles visibly tightened as she threw her head back at an unnatural angle.

"Reva," Crow whispered through tears.

"Look, sweetheart." Locasta walked behind Crow to whisper in his ear. "Watch as your beloved disappears."

Green pustules bubbled over Reva's face, popping, coloring her skin a greenish hue and leaving craters in their wake. Her nose elongated, twisted, making her look nothing like the female he knew, and the hands that had touched him with so much love extended into claws. A sickening snap filled the air as her spine arched, then curved in on itself. Finally, her body stilled as if she were sleeping. Every ounce of Reva's outer beauty had vanished beneath Locasta's curse, but Crow knew her heart. He knew that when she woke up again, she would still be his same fierce female, and he would love her regardless of what she'd become.

"Wait for it," Locasta squealed with excitement.

Reva's body flew upright with a gasp. Crow jerked toward her, but his restraints tightened. A weak, desperate sound escaped his throat. Reva patted her hands over her dark nightgown and looked up at Crow. Her emerald eyes, brighter than before, lifted slowly, landing on Crow with complete disinterest.

"Dance," Locasta ordered.

Reva immediately twirled through the room, hands stretched to the ceiling, her head reclined all the way back.

"Stop, Locasta. I'm begging you." Crow's voice cracked. Reva had just spent an entire day bringing their daughter into the world. She'd been exhausted and sore before the curse, but now... Crow felt a shadow of the pain Reva had to be experiencing deep in his bones. And she hated being told what to do. To be controlled like this, and by Locasta no less... "I'll do anything you want. Just... please..."

"All right," she cooed, then commanded Reva, "Come closer so he can have a good look at you."

Reva was instantly in front of them. Up close, it was worse than Crow could've imagined. The pustules left craters in her skin that oozed just enough to make them glisten. And they smelled—*Gods* how they smelled. Like death and decay. Her shoulders hunched, one higher than the other, and her hands—no, claws—were crooked and bent at every knuckle with black, pointed nails.

"Reva?" he breathed.

Her response was a cackling laugh that was *nothing* like the sweet rumbling sound Crow knew so well. His chest tightened, his heart crushed all over again. This was *his* fault. All of it. Damn his selfishness! He'd known Locasta would come for him eventually, yet he'd still brought Reva into hiding with him. Maybe if they had separated, none of this would've happened. Or, if he hadn't walked around his home unarmed, Locasta would be dead instead of Reva cursed and their daughter stolen.

"Don't worry." Locasta stepped between them and took Crow's face in her hands. The witch's eyes softened slightly, but the way her nails dug into his cheeks only reminded him that her anger would never be satiated. "I love you still, Crow, so I will grant you the mercy of Unknowing and curse you to the cornfield."

Crow's eyes widened and he gripped her wrists. The Curse of Unknowing didn't only make a fae forget something—it jumbled every tiny thought in their brain until they were little more than a slobbering creature. "Locasta, don't," he pleaded in a broken voice. He couldn't fix any of this if she took his mind.

Locasta simply smiled, her hands warm on his skin, blue light glowing in his peripheral vision. "One day you will be mine again."

The last clear thought in Crow's mind was how utterly sorry he was for everything.

Chapter Two

Reva

This still didn't feel completely real. Reva was *out* of the dark place—because of her daughter's magic. Thelia had believed she was a human named Dorothy but, before killing Langwidere, discovered who she truly was: a fae.

Reva took off her late sister's frilly pink dress and slid on the only other clothing in Glinda's wardrobe that wasn't a garish gown. It was a one-piece: pale pink—still hideous—with poofy sleeves and loose pants that clutched at her ankles. Losing her sister to Langwidere's horrific obsession with heads had wounded Reva deep down, but she knew Glinda would want her to mend the Land of Oz, to end the wickedness. And that was exactly what she would do—keep her chin up like she always had before.

"Ozma, are you ready?" Reva turned and asked her friend, who had swapped her own tattered blue dress for one of Langwidere's white gowns. This dress wasn't as seductive as the other choices but still had a sheer diagonal v in the back that went from neck to waist, highlighting the raised scar where

Ozma's wings had once been.

The one-piece itched at Reva's skin, but it was the only damn thing with pants that her sister seemed to own. Fortunately, it wouldn't be necessary for too long. She would swap it out for something else once they hit the brick road. Besides, she didn't want the distraction of Glinda to haunt her the whole journey. They may not have been thick as thieves, but they had loved and respected each other.

"Yes, I'm ready." Ozma ran a finger along her jawline, her bright blue eyes meeting Reva's emerald ones. "But I think you need to tell him you're leaving."

Reva clenched her jaw, trying not to bring herself to think about *him*. "No."

"No?"

"No." Reva peered down at Ozma's bare feet. "Still no shoes?"

Ozma wiggled all ten toes in the morning light spilling through the window. "Never." She handed Reva a leather satchel and placed another over her shoulder. Then she swiped her long blonde locks behind her back. "Plenty of goodies in there for the journey."

Reva pulled on her dark black boots—the one thing she still had left at Glinda's from the last time she'd stayed so long ago. She couldn't believe they were still here.

Reaching down by her waist, Ozma adjusted the dagger at her hip. Reva didn't need any weapon—she was her own weapon.

Reva walked to the door and quietly opened it, her eyes adjusting to the new lighting after being away from it so long. She halted as her gaze fell to a male body on the carpeted floor, curled on his side, asleep. Midnight locks, with dark feathers entwined, cascaded over his shoulders. Crow. He had always slept through anything.

Her heart didn't leap at the sight of him—she made sure of that. Reva narrowed her eyes, her magic beginning to crackle inside of her—a soft sound that only she could hear and feel. While down in the dark place, among trees that could move their limbs to rip one apart, and beasts that could do the same, she'd imagined hundreds of ways she would murder Crow when she saw him again. One of those ways was by her blasting lightning into his chest. Her magic had been gone then, but it wasn't any longer. Looking at him now, she thought of Thelia, and she could never follow through with it. Even though it was his fault Thelia had become Dorothy, his fault Reva herself had been turned into a cursed monster, his fault for not killing Locasta when he'd found out she was truly wicked.

Ozma pressed a hand to Reva's shoulder and cocked her head at Crow to wake him. With a quick motion, Reva placed a finger over her lips and waved her on. Ozma gave her a look that told Reva she disagreed with the choice she was making. She didn't give a fuck, not when the memory of Crow telling Reva not to use her powers against Locasta slipped into her mind.

Staying silent, they padded their way down the hall to the staircase and descended the wooden steps. At the bottom of the stairs, light shone down from the domed ceiling, casting its hue across a chaise and four chairs with white cushions. The room no longer contained Langwidere's dead body, Glinda's head, dead Wheelers, or the crack that had split the palace into two because of Thelia's magic. The palace's own magic, courtesy of Glinda, had mended the house, but Crow had done everything else. Cleaned the blood. Buried Reva's sister, Langwidere's heads, and the bitch's body.

A subtle movement caught Reva's attention. Waiting at the door with her arms crossed was Thelia. Her daughter. Her beautiful and caring daughter. Brown eyes—like Crow's. She was the spitting image of him, aside from Reva's ears and chestnut-colored hair. Even though Thelia's overalls were stained after a rinse, she was still wearing them. She had promised to go to one of the abandoned shops to find some new garments soon.

"So, you really are leaving without telling him?" Thelia

13

whispered.

Reva had asked her to meet them here for a temporary farewell, but she should have known questions would ensue. If anyone could make her turn around right now, it was Thelia, but Reva *had* to do this. If she didn't, their fates—Thelia's fate—could be destroyed by Locasta and Oz. The Wizard had the silver slippers and Ozma was going to make sure to get them back while Reva took care of Locasta.

"Yes," Reva finally said, "though I know you're going to tell him. At least give us a head start." That was all she needed, and she would make sure he couldn't catch up.

"I will stay silent until he asks." Thelia gnawed at her lower lip. "Which I can guarantee won't be long."

"I'll take it." He would sleep in if no one disturbed him.

Before Reva could say anything else, Thelia threw her arms around her, surprising Reva. She never would have expected for Thelia to embrace her so soon, but her daughter was different: more caring, more human. And she knew Thelia was this way, even from the little time they'd had with each other. Reva hugged her daughter in return, holding back the tears that were aching to come. But there would be no crying yet, not until they were tears of happiness after the Land of Oz was safe and free from the wicked. Then their world could prosper again.

"Take care of the South," Reva murmured in Thelia's ear.

"Tin and I will."

Tin... Reva didn't know him well. She only recalled him through her memories as the Wicked Witch of the West. The ones where she'd tried to murder him, murder them all.

A thrum to kill rocked through her, but not for the innocent—for another witch in the North, sitting daintily on her throne. Locasta would die for everything she'd done. Reva's lightning would burst the wicked one's heart to bloody pieces.

"I love you, Thelia," Reva whispered as she pulled back, calming herself with the knowledge that her daughter was safe, alive. For ten years within the dark place, she hadn't known. That uncertainty was part of what had made the hate for Crow fester. "When all of this is over, and Oz is safe, I look forward to getting to know you."

"I love you, too."

Ozma came closer and brought her arms around Thelia. "You will be a great ruler. I can feel the kindness of your heart." Thelia wasn't the only caring fae—Ozma had a tender heart as well.

Releasing Thelia, Ozma stepped back and allowed Thelia to open the door to the morning sunlight. She winced at the brightness.

Reva expected Crow to rush down the stairs, sliding his palm across the ornate banister to stop them. He didn't. And she was relieved.

Outside, the sun bore down on them, its heated rays making Glinda's clothing itchier against her flesh. In the distance, past the ivory and lilac flowers, the freshly turned dirt, where the heads of Langwidere were buried, stood out from the rest of the ground. She remembered the bitch, remembered how she'd changed Oz from a selfish human Wizard into a greedy, deranged Wizard. Langwidere had deserved to die. Oz would eventually be dead too—by Ozma's hand. The silver slippers would then be returned to their rightful owner.

"Calm down, my good witch," Ozma soothed in a low whisper. "I can practically see the smoke rolling off you."

It wasn't a lie. Reva could see light gray steam rising from her skin. She managed to hold it in before the lightning and thunder followed.

As they walked out the gate, Reva tried not to look at the pale pink statue of her sister. She gave Glinda a silent, final goodbye.

Reva and Ozma started down the yellow brick road. They took sugary pastries from their satchels and ate and drank their canteens of water along the way, only stopping to find a new dress for Ozma: a pale blue one with a rope belt around the waist.

There was nothing in the shop dark enough in color for Reva, and most appeared even more uncomfortable than what she was already wearing. She would deal with the pink and the itchiness a little longer.

While heading north along the yellow brick road, Ozma stared, mouth agape, at the world around them. The colorful trees, the cottages shaped like mushrooms, the winged bugs buzzing by.

Reva smiled to herself. She'd been trapped alone in that dark place for so long, for *years*, before a ray of light had fallen in—Ozma—illuminating the place with her words and her kindness. Seeing Ozma happy, *free*, after living in fear for so long, seeming like a completely different fae now that she was cleaned up, made her think back to how they'd met.

A loud crash sounded in the dark from not too far away. It was always dark here, but not to the point where Reva felt she were blind. It was in between the night and sunset. A rustle came from behind a blackened bush. Her magic still did not rise up to protect her, but she didn't care. She moved a branch to the side, spotting a blonde fae, her hair a tangled mess. The female's feet were bare, and a shredded tunic and pants covered the rest of her. Both garments appeared too small for her tall frame.

"Who the hell are you?" Reva snapped.

"I-I don't know," the fae stammered, sitting up and rubbing her eyes.

Perhaps this was an illusion, or a beast in disguise. But it couldn't be so, because a beast would have already tried to attack. They didn't trick here, and they didn't play nice or fair—they just wanted to tear one apart. No need for manipulation. "You don't know? Did you lose your memory or something?"

"No." The fae paused, staring down at her trembling hands. "I don't know. I was him and now I'm her. And I feel like her but I miss him."

Reva arched an eyebrow and took a step back. She had once been a fae who would've helped anyone in her territory of the West. But after the curse—the murders—she was hesitant to trust anyone in this nothingness of a place. She wouldn't have a problem killing this fae if she needed to. "What the fuck are you talking about?"

"I'm Tip." The female opened her eyes. "But I'm not Tip. I'm Ozma, the true ruler of Oz."

Reva scowled, studying the fae. "If what you say is true, you're not a ruler anymore. Not in this place."

"I didn't know. Not until Mombi. Not until Oz used the silver slippers…" Ozma turned away from Reva.

Reva didn't give a fuck about rulers, or Oz, or anything besides getting back to Thelia. She'd almost murdered her own daughter and Crow… Even if she hadn't killed them, she had slaughtered others. Lots and lots of fae. She could remember her claws digging deep into the flesh of innocents, then feeding the bloody pieces to her flying minions. But that hadn't been the true her. The transgression she couldn't get over though, was how she'd almost murdered her daughter. It was her one haunting regret.

Her gaze fell to Ozma's back, where the dress was ripped, and even in the barely-there light, a raised patch of skin caught her attention. From the wound, bright blood oozed over her skin, as if whatever used to be there had been cut off. Wings. Reva knew right away, and perhaps she'd been too harsh.

In the distance, a low, fierce growl reverberated through the trees. "You're going to have to get ready to run," Reva said.

"Why?" Ozma stood on her tiptoes and peered around a large tree trunk.

"The beasts will be coming, and they'll smell your blood. Not only them. Beware the trees covered in thorns—their limbs can move and capture you."

Ozma stared again at her hands, furrowing her brow. "My magic is gone."

"So is mine." It had been gone for years now. Some days she was grateful, some days she was angry, and some days she just wanted the repetitive cycle to end.

"We'll protect each other then?" Ozma asked, stepping toward Reva.

"Perhaps. It could be our best chance to survive." Reva wasn't sure how long she'd been in this place, but she knew it had been years.

The sounds drew closer, trees groaning, everything around them ravenous with hunger. Reva yanked Ozma forward, and they both took off at a sprint.

Reva shrugged off the memory as a new sound stirred from

all directions. *Squeak.* Unfamiliar. No. Not unfamiliar. She just hadn't heard it in years. They'd been followed.

"Seems like you'll see a living Wheeler for the first time." She should have known they would come, in need of a new master now that Langwidere was gone. The wheeled bastards should have returned to the edge of the Deadly Desert where they belonged, because she wasn't going to take care of them.

"Do you believe they're worth saving?" Ozma asked as the squeaking drew closer.

"No." She would have given them mercy if they'd chosen to leave the South already, but they didn't deserve to live now.

The squeals echoed from the forest on the sides of the brick road. Wheeler after Wheeler rolled out from behind the trees, their arms and legs too long for their bodies. Most were covered in dried blood and dirt, leaves in their rumpled hair. White ribbon stained with crimson blood sewed their lips shut. They arched their curving spines in an animalistic manner as they edged closer.

A female Wheeler with matted auburn locks of hair shot toward Ozma. The minion lifted a spiked wheel, the speed increasing, turning and turning. Ozma leapt up and caught a branch, easily scaling the tree. In the dark place, they'd both grown used to climbing up boulders and trees that weren't murderous to make an escape. Ozma may not have her full magic back yet, but Reva did.

Reva smirked as she easily dodged a male Wheeler who charged at her. A raised scar ran from a missing eye to the side of his head where a mangled ear hung. "You should have gone straight to the Desert," she said, clapping her hands together, creating a thunderous boom that not only vibrated within her but shook the ground.

Not taking her eyes from the Wheelers—who no longer moved toward her, their expressions startled—she sparked a bit of green light in the center of her palm. It crackled, sang, and began to ignite. Some of the Wheelers started to turn, but it was too late for any of them. A blast of lightning shot forward, electrifying the world around her.

Everything was green, green, *green*—like her skin had once been—until the color dissipated and only a flicker of yellowish light remained. Then there was nothing but smoke surrounding her and the scent of charred bodies.

Reva's gaze flicked up to Ozma who sat safely in the tree, staring down at her with her head tilted to the side.

"What?" Reva chuckled.

A frown formed on Ozma's face as she jumped from the branch. She swiftly pulled out the dagger from her hip and jolted toward a tree. A twitching Wheeler was pushing herself up at its roots. Ozma lifted the dagger and plunged it through the Wheeler's chest, directly into her heart. The Wheeler collapsed to her side, unmoving, crimson pooling from the wound as she stared blankly toward the trees.

"Missed one," Ozma said, daintily cleaning the blood from the blade with another Wheeler's tunic.

"I suppose you were tired of hiding in the tree and had to steal my *thunder*," Reva teased, but she was also satisfied that Thelia and Tin would be safer with many of the Wheelers gone. Another male, with obsidian feathers laced in his hair, crept into her mind, but she pushed the bastard away.

"I'm going to miss your sarcasm when we have to go our separate ways."

"I'll miss you too." Reva didn't want to think about Ozma not being by her side just yet. "Let's continue before we lose light."

CHAPTER THREE

CROW

Crow stretched his stiff back, letting out a quiet groan. Sleeping on the floor wasn't what had left him feeling so sore—he'd done that hundreds of times when there weren't any trees available to hang his hammock from. It was from sleeping on the floor after being knocked out of a tree by Wheelers, transforming into a broken bird, shifting back, cleaning up after Langwidere's death, burying her and dozens of heads, then waiting anxiously for Reva to open the damn door. Which she still hadn't done yet.

A million questions swirled through his mind. The most pressing one was where Reva had been all this time. *Trapped in darkness* was so vague, but Dorothy hadn't been told more than that. Surely, with more information, he could figure out what had happened when Dorothy broke the curse. It had been an extra advantage to her killing Langwidere, but the sudden appearance of Reva and her friend, Ozma, threw him off his game.

Crow *would* stick to questions about what had happened when Reva finally came out of her sister's old bedroom—even if it killed him not to make more personal inquiries. He hoped Reva was comfortable surrounded by Glinda's things after learning about her death. Crow hadn't seen the Good Witch since before Dorothy was born—she hadn't known Crow and Reva were together, and he'd had no other reason to visit—but time doesn't break familial bonds.

If Crow knew one thing about Reva's current feelings, it was that she seemed to loathe him with every fiber of her being. He couldn't blame her—and yet he *did* blame her. Crow settled his elbows on his knees and hung his head. Locasta had cursed her, taken away her daughter, but she had also cursed *him*. Taken *his* daughter. Reva had been completely aware of the risks when they'd gone into hiding together. Their entire relationship was spent with the threat of Locasta looming over them like a guillotine, its blade edging closer, but Reva had repeatedly assured him their love was worth the risk.

Crow ground his teeth together and shoved up from the floor. He would simply have to earn Reva back. Make up for everything that had happened. Somehow. Beginning with a nice, hot breakfast. It was a different meal than he'd meant to give Reva that fated night, but the thought was the same. Perhaps they could begin anew. Their daughter was back, their curses broken...

With fresh determination, Crow hurried down the stairs and through the foyer to the kitchen. Glinda's magic continued to keep the palace running even after Langwidere had killed her, and the room was full of baked goods. Stacks of buttery croissants, sticky buns, steaming muffins, and a variety of fruit-filled turnovers with syrupy filling covered the rose-gold marble countertops.

And, leaning over the various delicacies, loomed a shirtless Tin, his silver hair pulled back in a messy bun.

"Morning, *Father*," Tin said stoically without looking up from the turnovers.

Crow winced. Dorothy was far too good for someone like Tin—once a ruthless assassin with a stone heart. The Gnome

King's curse was broken, but something told Crow that Tin was broken too. It was going to take a lot to get over the fact that Tin had brought Dorothy back specifically to hand her over to Lion and Langwidere. It would be a lie to say Lion's path hadn't come as a surprise, that he would willingly kill the female who'd once helped him—*saved* him.

Crow would try to forgive Tin for Dorothy's sake, but if the bastard ever hurt his daughter, Crow would kill him without an ounce of guilt.

"Don't be a jackass," Crow grumbled. "Also, put on a shirt."

Tin smirked, the iron scar on his cheek pulling his skin with the movement. "You look like hell. Did you get any sleep?"

"Did *you*?" Crow threw back at him, then paused at the thought of *why* he wouldn't have slept. "No. Don't answer that."

Tin snorted and lifted a full plate of pastries. "Thelia already ate, so the rest is all yours. I'd hurry before they disappear."

Crow's stomach growled at the reminder of last night's dinner. After he'd dragged himself inside from burying heads, he'd just sat down to a plate of gravy-smothered chops when every piece of food had vanished. Magic kitchens weren't all they were cracked up to be. "Who is Thelia?"

"Your daughter," Tin replied as if it were completely obvious. "You talked last night, didn't you? She remembered her true name."

They had talked, but it was mostly about the task Reva had given Dorothy—no. *Thelia.* The name fit her so well, so perfectly, that he should've known who Tin was talking about the moment he'd said it. *Thelia, Thelia, Thelia.* The name echoed through his mind, dragging a knowing feeling from the depths of his memory. He'd almost thought it on the night of her birth, but then Locasta... He had begun to think Dorothy's true name was lost forever due to his curse. *Thelia.* He smiled to himself.

"Guess she didn't tell you," Tin muttered at his silence. "It was a long night, with a lot of life-changing shit, so don't go getting angry with her."

"I'm not." Her name was incredibly important, but not as pressing as other things. He moved around the kitchen counter. "I'm going to cook up some eggs and sausages." Assuming there were any, but Lion had lived in the palace only days ago. Given his vulgar hobby of chopping off heads, he struck Crow as a meat eater. Reva certainly was. It was something they bickered about at least once a week when they were together. She always wanted hot, filling breakfasts while he wanted something light, like a bowl of fruit or oats, and she refused to allow Whispa to make more than one meal—even if it was simply tossing some fruit into a bowl. Unfortunately for him, Reva was an early riser so she nearly always won. Crow grinned, remembering her victorious, smug smile when he would finally stumble down from the bedroom. It was a smile that left him eating whatever Whispa made instead of preparing his own meal. "Reva prefers heartier breakfasts."

Tin tensed. "You're making Reva breakfast?"

"Of course." He picked a large skillet off a hook on the wall.

"Umm. Happy cooking." Tin eased away from the pastries with his lips pulled back in a grimace. Then he spun on his heels and bolted from the room.

"Tin!" Crow yelled, but the other male was gone. Something about it was suspicious, but Tin was nearly impossible to figure out, so he turned back to the task at hand. Pulling his hair away from his face, Crow studied the two dozen cupboards. "If I were a mixing bowl, where would I be?" he mumbled to himself.

"Crow?" Thelia asked from the kitchen doorway.

A smile instantly spread across his face. "Good morning."

"Morning." She hurried to him and placed a kiss on his cheek. "Tin passed me in the hall and said you were up."

Crow nodded and motioned around the kitchen. "I want to make Reva breakfast. She and I need to talk a few things out."

Thelia stood silently beside him, eyes fixed on the floor, wringing her hands.

"Don't worry," he assured her. "You're safe now."

"That's not it," she said with a halfhearted smile.

"Is it about us leaving then? You seemed upset when you explained your mother's plan to travel. As much as I would love to spend time with you—and I know Reva does too—we need to fix Oz."

"I know."

"Trust me, your mother is extremely powerful, and I'll protect her with my life." Like he hadn't last time.

"Crow, stop talking," Thelia snapped, then sucked in a breath. "I'm sorry, I didn't mean to be harsh. It's just…" She exhaled, her eyes blinking one too many times.

Crow patted her shoulder. His daughter's entire existence was new to her, and he didn't want her to worry about hurting his feelings. "We've all been through a lot."

"She's gone," Thelia whispered.

His hand fell from her shoulder. That couldn't be right, could it? His stomach sank. "What do you mean?"

Thelia rubbed a hand over her mouth as if she regretted opening it. "I promised not to tell you, but the thought of Reva out there alone, crossing through the Emerald City to reach Locasta in the North, terrifies me. She and Ozma left together, but will be separating to go fight their own battles while I stay here as she requested. I can't lose her before I've had a chance to get to know her, especially after I somehow banished her to darkness when she was the Wicked Witch."

Reva left? *How?* When? He'd slept outside her door all night, specifically so she couldn't leave without him. It didn't matter if she wanted him to travel with her and Ozma. There was no way he was going to let Reva go to the North alone to face Locasta, especially when everything that had gone wrong in the past was because of him. If he had simply escaped the Northern palace and gone into hiding on his own… If he hadn't gone to Reva for help in destroying Locasta. And what good had it done? They'd failed to stop Locasta from brutalizing her citizens in the end.

Crow might not have magic that could inflict the same sort

of damage as Reva or Locasta, but he'd done more than train his brain over the last ten years. He'd learned how to fight, and fight well, so that one day he could take Locasta down himself. Reva coming back from the dead was never an option he'd thought possible, though he'd searched for answers about what exactly happened when Dorothy threw the water at the Wicked Witch. There was no record of a simple pail of water melting a faerie—even with the silver slippers, it had seemed strange to him. If he knew Reva hadn't been dead at all, he would've found a way to bring her back so they could destroy the Northern Witch together. Hell, he should've killed Locasta years ago when he ventured back to her Northern palace. His desperation to find the real Dorothy Gale had driven him to visit his ex-lover, but he hadn't been strong enough to fight her then. Escaping was the best he could do, and that hadn't come without sacrifices. His only ally in the palace—a human changeling Locasta kept as a pet—had created the distraction he needed to cross the border into the West. The man's agonized wails fading to deathly silence still echoed through Crow's mind.

"How long ago did she and Ozma leave?" he asked. His throat bobbed, his palms sweating, but he made sure to keep his voice even for Thelia's sake.

Thelia took Crow's hand in both of her own. "I'm sorry I didn't tell you sooner."

"I'm not angry with you," he promised. With Reva, yes, but not Thelia. "How long ago?"

"A few hours. It was just past dawn."

Crow nodded once, placed a kiss on his daughter's warm forehead, and left the kitchen.

"Where are you going?" Thelia called after him.

"To find your mother," he called back, and hurried to gather his belongings.

He was going to find Reva and keep her safe. Something he couldn't do twenty-one years ago.

Chapter Four

Reva

After two days of traveling on the yellow brick road in the Southern territory, Reva's endurance remained high. She was used to constantly being on the move in the dark place, avoiding the trees that would attack and hiding from the creatures that wanted to rip them apart. Some days in the dark place they could rest for longer than others, and that was when hope had been the loudest.

Reva and Ozma ate, slept, and chatted on their journey. They walked around the areas of the yellow brick road where the Wheelers had left their bloody victims, torn apart and mangled. None of the bodies were new, though—perhaps a few days old. The deaths only made Reva more determined to heal the Land of Oz.

To Reva, the grave markers she'd passed of Langwidere's victims were a true punch to the gut. The South wasn't supposed to be this way. She and Glinda's parents had owned this territory, kept it flourishing—Glinda had continued the tradition. And now it had gone to shit. The colorful cottages were still intact, but that didn't mean anything because mostly everyone had left or was dead. *The South isn't dead, though*, she told herself. The Southerners could return to make it thrive once more. Thelia could do it. Reva and Ozma would help if she needed them. She would *always* help her daughter.

"What are you scowling about now?" Ozma asked, bringing a bright red faerie fruit between her lips. Crunch. Crunch. *Crunch.*

Reva needed an apple, but they didn't grow in the South. They were her comfort. She had a lot going on in her head, too much, and she was tired of thinking about the Land of Oz and how broken it had become. She hadn't seen what the other territories looked like yet, but from what Thelia had told her, the East was run down, and the Emerald City was full of dangerous, destructive fae.

"You chew too loud," Reva said, avoiding the question.

"You're going to make me dig for the answer, aren't you?" Ozma smiled and glanced up at the moving clouds.

Reva sighed. "I know the rest of Oz is going to be even worse than this."

"This isn't so bad." Ozma's gaze connected with Reva's. She was a dreamer and always one to see the positive in everything. Ozma would probably even find the good in the Wheeler she'd stabbed through the heart by saying the fae was better off dead—which was true.

"I think all the headless fae buried across this territory would have to disagree."

"What I mean is," Ozma said slowly, "it can always be worse. Those deaths will not be for nothing. They are the start of something, and that includes Glinda."

Reva's chest tightened at her sister's name. As young fae, Glinda would parade around in her frilly pink dresses and Reva would wear dark clothing. Glinda was the light and Reva was the dark but neither were wicked—only their personalities were different. Glinda was bouncier, Reva more demanding, but both made their territories a priority and took care of them.

The memory of Locasta barreling into her room after Thelia was born crept into her mind. Reva could once again feel the cracking, twisting, and manipulation of bones, muscle, and skin. Her nose stretching and curving, the pustules bursting over her flesh, causing the green color to spread.

Clenching her jaw, Reva tucked away that anger to use later when the opportunity came. "You're right, this is the start of something."

It had been Reva and Ozma together for so long. Now she was ready to see the fae from the West, or at least the ones who had survived her wrath as the Wicked Witch. But that would have to wait, too.

It didn't take long before they entered the Eastern territory. There wasn't much to see besides forestry and *no apples*. They trekked farther and farther, and Reva kept her guard up for creatures that might attack, but all remained silent.

Right as the sunlight was about to die for the day, Reva spotted a small village. Blue and black cottages, along with larger buildings, were tucked and covered by pine trees on either side of the yellow brick road.

Lit lanterns guided their way as she and Ozma passed the buildings. In the triangular windows, flames bobbed atop candlesticks. Outside an inn, two fae, with curled horns atop their heads, held each other close and walked inside. Next door, a nymph stood in front of the entrance to a brothel, drinking out of a silver goblet. She glanced at Reva and Ozma when they drew closer.

"I know you," the nymph said, ticking her finger back and forth as she stepped into their path. Dark hair, with ribbon laced throughout, framed her delicate features, and a yellow dress of spider silk hugged her lithe form.

Ozma's eyebrows lifted in surprise. "You do?"

"No, no. Not you." The nymph shooed Ozma away and inched closer to Reva, pointing at the Good Witch's chest. "You. I've seen *you* before."

Reva watched as an unreadable expression crossed Ozma's face. Possibly disappointment? Even if Reva had met this nymph before, nobody would have recognized her friend since no one knew she existed. All the years she'd spent in Oz, she'd been Tip, not Ozma. Enchanted to look like a male to hide her identity and keep the Wizard of Oz in power. Mombi had been the one to do the Wizard's dirty work—she'd stolen Ozma away as a baby and raised her to not know who she really was. If Reva could snap *that* witch's neck right then, she would. But it was best no one knew who Ozma was yet—she was without her power and throne.

Reva squinted her eyes, not recognizing the nymph in the slightest.

The fae leaned in closely, her breath reeking of ale. "You're Reva. How are you back? You're not monstrous anymore either."

The blood coursing through Reva's veins came to a halt. She couldn't breathe. With hurried motions, she grasped the nymph by her shoulders and shoved her against the outside wall of the brothel, knocking over a clay pail.

"Keep your mouth shut," Reva whispered, the lightning within her already crackling, creating waves of thunder in her ears. "It was a curse and the curse is gone."

"Reva," Ozma warned.

"Don't worry." The nymph smiled, not the least bit afraid. "No one will recognize you in these parts. Most who live here have never been to the West. But I was at Glinda's palace when *you* last visited, remember?"

Releasing the nymph's shoulders, Reva's brow furrowed. That would have been twenty-two years ago. The last time she'd gone to Glinda's palace, she'd only stayed the day and was supposed to return the next season, but had never gotten the chance. Things had heated around Oz because of the witch in the East, Inora. The Eastern Witch would slaughter anyone who came into her territory who wasn't from there, including families

29

of Easterners who visited. But the last time Reva had walked into Glinda's room, she remembered her sister being pleasured by— "Oh, you were the one in her bed!" The nymph's hair had been in a braid that day, and she'd been naked except for a pink glittering choker.

"How is Glinda by the way?"

"She's..." Reva shook her head.

The nymph seemed to understand as she nodded with melancholy sparkling in her eyes. "And Langwidere?"

"Dead."

"Good."

"We need a place to stay for the night," Ozma said, peeking through the window, lips parted in surprise.

The nymph stared at Ozma's odd motions and turned back to Reva. "I'm Falyn."

The name—she'd heard it recently. Reva lifted a dark brow. "You gifted Dorothy a machete. She saved the South."

Falyn gave a small smile. "I knew she would do something great again." She turned, opened the brothel door, and motioned them forward. "Well, come on. Enough chit-chat because I have money to be making."

They followed Falyn inside the brothel, where sex and incense filled Reva's nose. Her body normally would have tightened at the scent but she was too drained to feel aroused. She hadn't had a lover in years. Yet there had been the nights where she'd been asleep, high up in a tree in the dark place, and dreamt of Crow. His hands on her waist, sliding up to cup her breasts. Him so tender, her so wild. His mouth on hers, her fingers drifting down to—

Fuck Crow, she thought, shaking off the images stirring within her. She focused on several shot glasses on a counter filled with golden liquor. Grabbing one, she tossed the liquid into her mouth and relished the burn as it glided down her throat.

Reva glanced at Ozma, who stared with wide eyes at the fae around her. Some of them were naked, straddling males as they played games at the tables. Other males were mounting lovers against the walls. She smiled and nudged Ozma's arm. "Don't act like you're so innocent. I know you've seen a naked male before."

"Only myself when I was Tip. Then Jack..." Ozma drifted off, and Reva knew she was thinking about her true love.

"Now you've seen more." Reva's gaze carried throughout the room as she followed the nymph toward a hallway. Paintings covered the wall of lovers fucking. Prostitutes and their clients appeared as if they were trying to mirror the positions depicted.

Ozma didn't look surprised anymore. She seemed inquisitive while watching the females and the males together, as if she were attempting to learn how it all worked.

"It will come naturally when you reunite," Reva whispered to Ozma as they turned down a hall filled with rooms and crimson curtains as doors.

"Would you like me to get either of you some company for the night?" Falyn asked while lifting one of the curtains leading into a room with a single bed and dresser.

"No, but would you have a change of clothing?" Reva pulled out a ring from her satchel. "Something black." She'd been ignoring the itching of the clothing but she couldn't handle it anymore.

Falyn waved the ring away. "Only if you replace it with what you're wearing. That clothing is far more valuable than anything I own.

"Are you sure?"

"Trade for anything in the closet you wish. I'm going to work for the remainder of the night, but you two can rest here." Falyn spun around to leave, but stopped to glance over her shoulder. "I'm glad you're back. Glinda mentioned what a wonderful leader and sister you were."

Reva didn't say anything—her fists tightened at what Langwidere, Locasta, and the Wizard had set into motion.

Chest heaving, Reva turned to find Ozma sitting on the bed,

peering down at her hands. "What is it?"

"I just want to get back to him." Ozma sighed. "I've always wanted to get back to him."

Sometimes Reva wanted to roll her eyes because Ozma was more than who she used to be. She hadn't known she was the ruler of Oz—not until she'd broken free from Mombi's curse, then had been cast away to the dark place because of the Wizard. And now, there was so much more for Ozma than a single fae male. "You've known what"—Reva shrugged—"four fae your whole life before meeting Thelia and the others? Mombi, Oz, Jack, and me. I know Jack will be happy to see you from what I've heard of him, but you also have a whole new path now. It might not be a path that Jack would ever choose to walk."

"The Jack I know would. But I'm more concerned about my body." Ozma motioned at her breasts. "What if he doesn't like it? What if he doesn't like *me* anymore?"

"You did say he doesn't have a preference between males and females, so why wouldn't he? And if he doesn't, then fuck him. You're Ozma, Queen of Oz." Reva would strike Jack down with her magic if need be.

Ozma bit her lip.

Reva pressed her hands on Ozma's narrow shoulders. "When the sun rises, go to him and warn him about the Wizard. I'll be fine. After I deal with Locasta, I'll wait for you in the Emerald City and help you claim the palace. But if you arrive and there's still war over the territory, go back to Thelia in the South."

"I'll meet you there." Her blue eyes met Reva's, gleaming with determination. "Unless you need my help with Locasta first."

"No, you can't. Not with her ability to change you into something else. That's why I had Thelia stay at the Southern palace—we can't all be in the same place at the same time. If something happens to me, there will still be the two of you."

Ozma pressed her hand to her chest. "I only had my wings

for moments, but I wish I had them now to help."

"You'll grow a new pair once you get the silver slippers. The shoes' magic will yield to you in whatever way you wish." The way Thelia had wanted Reva gone... Even though Thelia should have wanted her truly dead for everything Reva had done.

Ozma nodded and pulled back the red satin sheets. "Let's get some rest."

Reva removed her boots and slipped beneath the covers, but she couldn't shut her thoughts off. "Do you know what you're going to say to Jack when you see him?"

"I've gone over it a thousand times in my head, and I still don't have an answer. I still miss being Tip at times, but perhaps that's because I know Jack loved him. But I love myself now. I just hope Jack can too." Ozma stretched and closed her eyes, breathing slow and even.

Reva shouldn't have brought up the subject, because now she couldn't stop her thoughts from turning to her past lover and how they had first met.

Reva strolled down to the market because she preferred to pick her fruit herself. It had to be perfect. Not too soft, not too hard. She bid a passing hello to every fae she encountered on the way, only stopping to tickle a young brownie beneath her chin.

Merchants filled their stands with goods—dark clothing, obsidian jewelry, and fruit. Her favorite fruit stand caught her eye. Apples and oranges rested in baskets along the counter. Beneath the afternoon sun, a perfect green apple sparkled. That was the one. She reached for the luscious piece of fruit, but a male's hand grabbed it first.

Reva narrowed her eyes at him, first for stealing her apple, and second because he wore a mask shaped like a bird's head that covered half his face. Black hair with feathers entwined fell past his shoulders. "You're not from around here," she accused.

"How do you know?" he asked, cradling the apple closer to his chest, his brown eyes flashing impishly from beneath the mask.

"Because I know everyone in this territory." She looked at the stand's owner, Yovey, who was busy talking to another customer. His gold ring-

covered fingers flashed as he gestured toward his fruit.

The stranger lifted his mask over his head, revealing a handsome face that made her catch her breath. He had a chiseled jaw, a light scar running across his nose, and high cheekbones. Reva came back to herself, not one to be swayed by a pretty face. She'd had plenty of those in her bed.

He arched a brow. "Every single one?"

"Every single one." Reva named each owner and customer at the stands circling the area, reciting the monikers like a shopping list. She held out her hand, palm up. "Now give me my apple."

He tossed the apple into the air and caught it again. "I was planning on bringing it to the Western Witch, Reva—I hear she favors pristine fruit."

Her eyes narrowed.

"And why's that?" She didn't do well with strangers entering her or her sister's territory—not with the Eastern Witch becoming more and more deceptive. Inora had already sent spies on multiple occasions, so the arrival of an outsider was never a good sign. If she had to kill him right then and there, so be it.

"Why does she like pristine fruit or why am I bringing her some?" he asked with a playful smile.

"The latter."

He shrugged. "I need to discuss a Northern problem with her, so I was hoping it would help put her in a helpful mood."

A Northern *problem? What was Locasta up to now? Everyone believed the bitch to be good, but Reva could see through her lies. She just couldn't prove anything—yet. Locasta wasn't like Inora, who didn't care about showing the Land of Oz who she truly was.*

"You want Reva?" She cocked her head. "Go to her palace, then."

He dropped the apple into her palm. "Do you really believe I wouldn't recognize you, Reva?"

Reva had never been caught off guard. Not until right then. "Who the fuck are you?"

"You can call me Crow."

"What do other people call you?" she asked.

"Crow. Though, I suppose it depends on who you ask," he said with a wink.

34

"I'm leaving," Ozma whispered, rousing Reva from sleep before kissing her on the cheek. "We will meet again soon."

"Stay safe, Ozma." Reva's heart beat faster, missing her friend already. "I know you can do this. You're strong and determined, and Jack will fall in love with you all over again when he sees you. It doesn't matter that your body is different. He will see *you*."

"I hope so." Ozma bit her lip. "Now, try not to be too hard on Crow."

Crow...

Ozma smiled, pushed back the curtain, and left. Reva was alone again, as she had been in the dark place before Ozma had arrived. But this was for the better. Going after Locasta would be dangerous, and Reva didn't want anyone else to suffer from the witch's vicious curses.

She sat up and quickly removed Glinda's one-piece pink outfit to leave on the bed for Falyn, then walked to the wardrobe in the corner. Ropey vines were etched into the wood and heavy brass handles accentuated the doors. Reva pulled the doors open to sift through the nymph's clothing. She found black leather pants, a corset, and a tight tunic with lace around the collar and the ends of the sleeves. When she turned over the shirt, there were ribbons crisscrossed in the back. It was *perfect*.

Just as Reva finished sliding on the clothing and buttoning the front of the tunic, Falyn entered the room, wet-haired and more than a little rumpled.

"I would have returned sooner," Falyn said, "but my client paid me for the entire night and multiple rounds. I do hope he returns, because he was *exquisite*."

Reva ground her teeth as she thought about something distasteful. Crow's mind had been back for ten years—had anyone else found *him* exquisite?

"Something wrong?" asked Falyn.

"No, only thinking about the journey ahead," Reva replied, dropping her scowl and picking up her pack to head back out.

Falyn lifted Glinda's garment and hugged it to her chest. "I'm not sure I'll see you again, but stay safe. The Emerald City isn't as it once was."

Reva told Falyn goodbye, passing couples buried deep in each other as she left the brothel to venture north once again on the yellow brick road. The sunlight revealed that the road wasn't as pristine here as it was in the South, its color faded to a dull mustard.

The farther she traveled out, the worse the road became. Cracks in bricks, some missing, others uneven. She'd been traveling for too long when she stopped to eat berries and drink from a glistening stream. Brushing her hands clean against her pants and filling her canteen with more water, she spun around as a loud clicking noise reverberated off the trees. Whatever it was, it didn't sound small.

Reva's magic thundered, and she crept around a tree trunk. As she took a step forward on a bed of leaves, a crack echoed and she flew up off the ground, screaming. Iron-spun ropes with tiny holes surrounded her, the net swaying gently. It had been hidden by leaves—one that was used for hunting. The iron burned her hands and rendered her powerless.

"Fuck!" she shouted.

A rustle stirred the bushes, drawing her attention. Out came a harmless water fae with gills on the side of its neck, making the same clicking sound before darting on all fours into the river.

Trapped in iron with no one else around, Reva's only hope was for someone to pass by and help before she grew too weak and became something's prey.

CHAPTER FIVE

CROW

Crow trudged along the yellow brick road as dawn filtered through the trees. For fae who'd only gotten a few hours' head start, Reva and Ozma hadn't wasted a second. He'd pushed himself to walk faster, and sleep less, just to close the gap between them, but it had been three days. Given that Reva hadn't visited the Southern woods for decades, Crow figured she would keep mostly to the path. And that would lead to the same town where he'd finally found Thelia and Tin.

How ironic, he thought as he glimpsed a white-washed building. He would soon be asking around town for Reva instead of his daughter. It seemed Reva and Thelia had something in common—running, unknowingly, from him. Though Reva should've known better. There was no chance he would let her run off to fight Locasta alone.

He paused across the street from the brothel and set his pack on the ground to stretch. There were only a few places he could enter this early—eateries, galleries, and trade shops wouldn't open for another hour or so—which left the inn and the brothel.

"Hello," a nymph called brazenly from an upstairs window.

Ah, shit. With his luck, Reva had spent the night in town and would emerge just in time to see him chatting up a prostitute. "I'm not looking for company, thank you," he called back.

"Are you sure I can't—"

The front door opened and a petite blond female emerged. She wore a simple blue dress, no longer one of Langwidere's. *Ozma*. "Fucking finally," he whispered to himself. But where was Reva?

The true ruler of Oz stared at him from across the road for a long moment before moving toward him. He felt frozen in place. If he moved, would she change her mind about approaching? Run and tell Reva they'd been found?

"Good morning," Ozma said cheerfully. She stopped in front of him and met his gaze. "It took you long enough."

He wasn't sure if that was an accusation or not. "I'm sorry?"

Ozma picked nervously at her skirts. "I... shouldn't be talking to you."

"Why's that?" he asked, as if he didn't know.

"Reva doesn't want you to go to the North with her." Her gaze fell to the ground. "I knew you were following us so I pretended to leave on my own mission first. I stayed behind to catch you even though..."

Crow waited for her to continue but only silence stretched between them. His heart went out to her—Reva was her friend. They'd survived some dark place together. And now, she was betraying that bond they'd built.

"I only want to protect her," he reassured Ozma. "Reva can't take on Locasta alone."

Ozma nodded. "That's why I stayed back. We survived too much for her to get herself killed so recklessly."

Crow swallowed a dozen questions about what exactly they'd survived. Where they had been. What was Reva like now? It had been *decades*...

"She went that way." Ozma pointed down the yellow brick

road. "If you hurry, you'll catch up to her by midday."

Crow swept his pack off the ground and quickly flung it over his back. The movement sent his mask sliding down from the top of his head to cover his face. "Thank you," he said in a rush. "Truly. Thank you."

"Don't thank me." Ozma sounded torn, but determined. "Just keep her safe."

"You have my word." He lifted her hand and planted a kiss on her knuckles. Then he took off after Reva with renewed energy.

Crow didn't slow his pace—not until he, finally, caught his first glimpse of Reva. The sight of her sent his pulse racing. She had ditched the pink one-piece outfit in favor of a black-lace tunic and leather pants. Seeing her in her favorite color again hit Crow with a wave of nostalgia. His body yearned to step out of the alley and go to her. He missed the days when they would walk side by side—arguing, touching, laughing, touching some more.

But it was nothing like old times. He would do whatever it took to make things return to how they'd been, to when she'd loved him, but first he had to find the courage to speak to her.

She was bent near the river, cupping water in her hands to drink. The sun beat down, caressing her long hair, and making the water behind her sparkle. She looked so magical. So lethal and beautiful. How had he ever gotten so lucky to win the heart of such a female?

Drawn forward by her presence, Crow stepped off the crumbling yellow brick road. A twig snapped underfoot, and he cringed. Reva would attack if she thought someone was sneaking up on her. He cleared his throat to call out to her, but stopped himself at the last moment. Announcing himself could send her running—being attacked would bring her right to him. And maybe help her work out some of the anger she clearly carried for him.

Before he could make a solid decision, another, louder snap echoed through the forest. At first, he thought he'd stepped on an entire pile of sticks. Then the sound was followed by Reva's scream. Crow's blades shot out from beneath his bracers, arching over his hands like claws, as he prepared to slay any dangerous fae that threatened her.

What Crow found instead stopped him in his tracks. Reva hung from a tree in a large iron net. His first instinct was to rush over and save her, as much as she would hate that, but he retracted his blades, chuckling silently. The indignity of it had to be killing her.

Crow's chuckle slowly gave way to a mischievous grin. Reva would *have* to speak with him if she wanted to get down. The question was, should he approach her now or wait until she was truly desperate to escape?

The answer was simple, though. She had suffered enough because of him and, while he needed her to hear him out, he wouldn't purposely terrify her. There was no telling what horrors she'd experienced over the last two decades, first as Locasta's monstrous puppet and then wherever she'd gone after the curse broke.

"Who the fuck is there?" Reva called as Crow strode toward her. Even trapped in a net, she didn't seem to be frightened of whatever predator prowled the forest.

"That depends." Crow paused beneath the net and waited for it to spin slowly around so she could see him. When she did, her face quickly morphed from shock to anger—likely because he had followed her, though perhaps also because she hadn't noticed that he was doing so. "Would you rather someone else save you?" he asked with a chuckle.

"Don't you dare leave me here," she seethed.

Crow made a show of releasing his blades and walking up to where the net met the tree trunk, then paused. "If I let you down, we'll talk?"

Reva mumbled something unintelligible, her eyes narrowing, and a harsh scowl formed on her face. "Why are you here?"

He wanted to admit that Ozma was worried about Reva but didn't want to cause a rift between them. Ozma had clearly felt disloyal when she'd found him. Instead, he pointed a finger playfully at Reva in the net. "You're as light on your feet as always, my love, and rather quick too. I didn't hear you leave your room at Glinda's which put me hours behind, yet it still took me days to catch up."

"I snuck out for a reason," she spat.

Crow shrugged as if it meant nothing, though he felt like a fire ignited in his chest. "I'm well aware that you wanted to avoid my 'tagging along.' I'm not stupid—my curse was broken too."

"Are you sure about that? It seems like you're having trouble taking a hint." The chains creaked and groaned as the net swayed.

Crow snorted. "That's nothing new, is it?"

"Far from it," Reva admitted. "Maybe if I'd been blunter before leaving Glinda's, none of this would've happened."

"It would've only endeared you to me more."

Her gaze shifted toward the sky and she let out a loud breath through her nose. "Get lost, Crow," she finally said.

He smiled and took a few steps away. Even now, she was as feisty as he remembered. "If you insist."

"I deserve to kill Locasta for what she did to me and to Thelia!" Reva shouted, her emerald eyes boring into him. "*I* deserve it! And *I* deserve to do it on my own terms."

He knew she was right. Locasta had been his burden to bear until he'd asked for Reva's help. Perhaps he should've stayed and taken Locasta's abuse so the females he loved would've never known so much pain. But then Thelia wouldn't have been born. Neither he nor Reva could've known the outcome of his trip to see the Good Witch of the West—the love that would blossom between them—but, regardless, he was the one who had brought Locasta's wrath down on Reva. Crow took a steadying breath and quickly sliced the rope surrounding the nearby tree branch.

Spinning, he caught Reva in his arms, net and all. The iron burned his fingers but he found it hard to care as he clutched her tightly. It had been too long since he held her. "Reva," he breathed.

"Put me down," she growled, twisting in his arms and batting at the iron.

"Sorry." Crow set her on her backside and helped peel the net away. "Are you okay?"

"Just wonderful." She stood and blew a piece of ruffled hair from her face. "Now if you'll excuse me."

Crow swept an arm out to let her by, then promptly followed on her heels.

"That wasn't an invitation, Crow."

He laughed. "Since when have I ever needed one?"

"Crow—"

"Reva." He grabbed her hand and pulled her to a stop. She quickly yanked it out of his grip. "I understand why you're angry. I do. But Locasta came after our family because of *me*. If this is your fight, your … revenge, then it's mine too. You want to be the one to kill her? Fine. But I have my own vengeance to chase. It will benefit us both if we work together and, if I have the chance to make things right between us, all the better."

"There *is* no making things right," Reva gritted through a clenched jaw. Emotion flickered in her gaze for a brief second, then disappeared. She scanned him up and down. "You want to come? Then keep up. I won't wait. And I get to kill the bitch when we find her."

"Fair enough." They would be stronger together. Safer. He hurried after Reva as she started for the road again. "I can't fly anymore, but I'm more than capable of matching your pace."

"Can't fly?" She looked at him over her shoulder with narrowed eyes.

Crow shrugged. "I was looking for the human Dorothy and… Locasta didn't like that very much. My other form is completely useless now." Not that it had been any good the night

Thelia was born.

Reva faltered. "Why didn't you get one of the Wizard's cures?"

"Oz destroyed them all before he disappeared."

"Like hell he did," Reva barked. "The only thing more important to him than his precious *medicines* is faerie fruit."

Could that be true? He'd gone to the Emerald City for a cure right after Locasta broke him, but the guards had turned him away to protect the Wizard's reputation. When he'd gone to the tavern to drown his many sorrows, the other patrons told him tales of Oz's outbursts—including one that destroyed all his potions. He'd been so disheartened at the time and the dryad had sounded so sure when she'd relayed the information. But if there was a chance the rumors were wrong—a chance they were really still in the palace....

"We have to go to the Emerald City," he said in a hoarse voice.

"Fuck no. I won't delay my vengeance."

"It will actually take us less time to cross through the Emerald City than it would to go around it," he reasoned.

Reva cast him a hard stare over her shoulder. "I may have only been back a few days, but I've heard what the capital is like now."

"If we can't survive the city unscathed, how will we hope to survive Locasta?" he asked. Then, without waiting for her to reply, added, "I need some of Oz's potions to heal my other form."

"You should have gotten them long ago."

"Reva." His voice cracked and he slammed his jaw shut. He wouldn't beg—if she insisted on heading straight to the North, he would go with her and get the cure after they killed Locasta.

She slowed her steps for a moment. "Fine. Since it's faster than going around."

A relieved breath fell from his lips. They had both already suffered so much over the years, and if there was a chance for his bird form to heal…

"Wait!" He quickly caught up to her, questions about the dark place burning inside him. "Thelia told me that her magic sent you somewhere else. What was it like?"

Reva pressed her lips into a tight line. "It doesn't matter. I'm here now."

But Crow knew that it *did* matter. It mattered very much.

CHAPTER SIX

REVA

Crow can't fly.

Reva told herself not to care about his strong, elegant bird wings being useless. Again, because of the Northern Witch... He'd asked about the dark place, and in that moment, she'd wanted to tell him, but she couldn't. She wasn't ready to speak of it to anyone, least of all him.

For now, they would need to cut through the Emerald City to gather potions to help Crow. To be honest, she didn't want to leave his bird form broken, but that didn't mean she wanted them to go together. Perhaps Glinda would have said Reva was being too harsh on him. Perhaps Thelia would have agreed. Perhaps Ozma would have said forgiveness was the answer. The old Reva would have fucked him right against the nearest tree trunk. But this wasn't then, this was now. She'd been a cursed, monstrous creature who slaughtered fae after fae, and she could forgive herself—and him—for that. But because of Crow, her daughter had been taken away from her.

Thelia could have died. There were so many times her life

could have dissolved—a simple snap of the neck from Locasta was all it would have taken. In the human world, she could have met any number of unknown fates. Or worse, Langwidere could have been wearing Thelia's fucking head right now if Thelia hadn't drawn up her magic and defeated the bitch. All of this was because of Crow's scorned ex-lover—Locasta. The Northern Witch's vendetta against Crow. Reva wasn't an idiot—she knew it wasn't completely Crow's fault. But it didn't make things—or her—feel any better. Reva hadn't gotten to spend more than a few hours with her daughter.

Something green slid in front of Reva's face, interrupting her thoughts. It was round and bright. Her eyes shifted to the glistening apple. The perfect firmness. No bruises, no dents— the faerie fruit would taste divine.

Reva wanted to slap the apple out of Crow's hand and make him hurt again, make him feel the pain she'd felt while in that dark place before Ozma had come. But she was selfish in that moment, she was greedy, and she was *hungry*. So instead, she ripped the fruit from his grasp and pressed the apple in between her lips to bite into it. The sweet liquid drizzled out onto her tongue. Almost as good as sex.

"You're welcome," Crow said, fighting a smile while he watched her take another bite.

A cool breeze ruffled the ends of her hair as she side-eyed him with no reply and continued on. Reva wondered if he'd walked this same path with Thelia when her daughter had first come to Oz. She knew her silence couldn't last all of her immortal life, because she had questions.

Reva finished the apple and tossed the core along the edge of the yellow brick road. A swarm of tiny faeries flew from the foliage to finish off the core.

Taking a breath, Reva looked past the blooming trees at the clouds in the distance. "What was Thelia like?" She paused, her nails digging into her palms. "When you first met her?"

Crow didn't miss a beat, as if he'd been expecting the

question. He had always known her better than anyone. "Even though the curse made it impossible to think clearly, I remember every moment I spent with her." He rubbed a hand against his jawline. "When I first met Thelia in the corn field, she wasn't frightened in the least. She was strong-willed and determined like you, a thinker like me. As a child, she already seemed fit to rule."

From the brief moments Reva had spent with Thelia, she felt he was right.

Another thing nagged at her, and she knew it would only bring about anger, but she chose to be a glutton for punishment anyway. "Why didn't you *tell* her who she was? After your curse was broken, you could have *told* her."

Crow inhaled deeply through his nostrils and shook his head. "Would it have made her life any better? Thelia was a child. Can you imagine telling a child that they killed their own mother? Young fae adjust differently, but she was raised as a human. It would have destroyed her at that age. As much as you hate it, Thelia had a home already, a life. People who loved her."

Reva curled her hands into fists, the lightning sparking off them as she slowly turned to face him. "Did you know when she went back to the human world, they thought she was mad? They poked and prodded her to try and make her better! When there was nothing wrong with her to begin with!"

Crow's eyes widened and his throat bobbed. "She—she didn't tell me about that."

"The people who raised her did it because they thought she was crazy and that it would help her." She held up a hand before he could interrupt. "And you know what Thelia told me: if she wasn't fae, the process could have either killed her or left her mind like yours was when you'd been cursed. Only, for Thelia, the damage would have been permanent."

"I only did what I thought was right for her." Crow's eyes glistened, his dark hair falling forward. "We all make mistakes."

"You more than anyone." Reva charged away from him before she spat out more than she wanted to—about wishing she

47

hadn't met him. But that would be a lie… Thelia would never have been born. And she didn't let herself think about the good moments between them either.

He grabbed her by the elbow, turning her to face him. "You've made mistakes too, Reva. It was *your* idea for us to hide in that house despite the number of fae living nearby who could see us. It was *your* idea not to have any guards with us for the birth. So you can't blame everything on me." He jabbed at his chest. "But you know what? I don't blame you. Because, like I said, we all make mistakes."

"Yet you brought it up." A part of her knew Crow was right, that it was her fault too. But that raging other part of her held on tighter. She'd been in that dark place for too long, and it still held onto a piece of her, more than the curse had.

"I—"

"Just stop talking," she said with a sigh, "and let's hurry so we can make it to the Emerald City sometime tomorrow."

Crow didn't say a word, only clenched his jaw and walked beside her.

Reva wondered how the Emerald City would look now. Thelia had told her what she'd seen from afar. It would be dangerous, especially if they went to the palace, but Reva was already used to that. She had her magic, and she could outrun almost anything.

They continued traveling for a long while, and she studied all the scenery they passed, trying to recall if it had changed since she'd been gone. It all seemed like a blur of greenery in her memories now.

As the light in the sky lessened, and the clouds turned gray from a storm brewing, Reva couldn't keep her mouth shut any longer. On the journey, they'd only stopped to eat and relieve themselves. Neither one had spoken another word to each other. She didn't know why it irritated her that he'd listened to her and stayed silent, but it did.

"So, how many people did you fuck while I was away?" she

asked, her tone accusing.

Crow stilled, his gaze sliding to hers. "I'm not going to dignify that with a response."

She cocked her head as an influx of emotions rocketed through her. Hurt. Jealousy. Bitterness. "That many then."

Loud hooting blared in the distance, leaving Crow with his mouth hanging open, his words trapped inside. She knew that familiar sound, just as she knew the feel of her own heartbeat.

The storm clouds were blowing in faster than expected, quickly eclipsing the sky. A loud boom of thunder cracked and trembled above them.

The rumbling set the cursed pixies into a screeching frenzy. They had once belonged to her—another creation courtesy of Locasta—and helped the cursed Reva to do her merciless bidding. She remembered Whispa, her loyal friend, becoming the first of the night beasts. Her heart got stuck in her throat at remembering seeing what Whispa had become, flying Thelia away. Whispa had been with her family for years, and now Reva didn't know what had become of her.

The Emerald City was only a few hours away now, but she and Crow wouldn't make it before the darkness swallowed them whole—not even close.

One of the advantages the cursed pixies had was their keen hearing. And she knew they would recognize her scent, even if she wasn't the same wicked green creature anymore. Reva could control them back then, but she couldn't now.

She whirled to face Crow. "Shift!"

His gaze searched the tops of trees. "I can't fly. And even if I could, I wouldn't be able to carry you."

"You don't need to!" The cursed pixies were fast and they would arrive any moment. She knew just where to go and it would be much faster to carry him, while leaving the pixies with less opportunity to harm him. They were only small specks right now, but they were gaining speed. "Shift!"

In a flash of black smoke, as if his fae form had never been,

Crow stood with one foot on the ground in his bird form. He ruffled his obsidian feathers, one wing hanging limply. Reva quickly scooped him up as the cursed pixies drew closer, their hoots echoing straight to her marrow.

Crow remained quiet, but his body fidgeted when she drew him to her chest. "This is as close to me as you're ever going to get again."

As the darkness set in and soft sprinkles hit her skin, Reva scurried from the yellow brick road and headed into the forest to where she'd last relieved herself. Deeper and deeper, pushing branch after branch out of the way, she searched for the shelter she'd seen earlier. Just up ahead rested a gray mound of rock with a wooden chimney and matching door. She didn't know if anyone was home—she didn't care either.

Around her and Crow, the hooting turned into vicious screeching. The cursed pixies, with their skeletal forms and elongated arms, surrounded her, swarming and swarming. Reva's thunderous magic roared through her veins, and the emerald lightning crackled onto her free palm. She flicked her left arm to the side, tossing a bolt of lightning at a beast baring its fangs, burning it to a crisp as it howled. Another pixie came, then another. But not as many as she'd thought would attack. Some appeared confused, their wings pumping in the air, their bodies unmoving, as though they didn't know if they wanted her to be their master once more or if they wanted to kill her for controlling them in the first place. Others didn't seem to care as one's claws struck the flesh of her neck and another sliced the top of her hand.

She spun the lightning so that it spread and spread, cocooning her and Crow within its depths. The cursed pixies jolted forward, bouncing off the current, too stupid to realize it would lead to their deaths. Sprinting forward, Reva dropped her magic when she reached the door to the rock mound. She turned the knob, finding it unlocked, and threw herself into the dark home before slamming the door shut with her boot. Chest heaving, she set Crow on the stone floor and a moldy scent hit her nose.

The cursed pixies screeched and raged on the opposite side of the door. Reva let a spark of lightning flicker in the center of her palm as she scanned the abandoned shelter. Whoever had once lived here must not have been around for years. Cobwebs and dust coated a wooden table without chairs. A feathered mattress with holes and a blanket was against a rocky wall. Broken cups were strewn across the dirt floor. Two logs rested in the fireplace in the back, and there seemed to be no other rooms.

Reva tossed a few sparks of her magic at the logs, flames instantly catching and rising.

The cursed pixies' cries still hadn't stopped. Rapid scratching came at the door, making her flinch. In the distance their wild howls continued, accompanied by pained screams—some of the cursed pixies must have found other victims to satisfy their hunger. A sense of guilt washed over her that this was happening to innocent fae because she'd led them here.

Crow still stood on the ground near the door, seeming to guard it. In that form, he wouldn't be able to fight off anything.

Reva pressed her hands on her hips. "You can shift back now."

In the glowing light of the fire, his brown eyes met hers, and he shook his small head. A low caw escaped his dark beak.

Her brow furrowed as she crept closer. "You never had a problem shifting back before."

With a tilt of his head, he used his beak to ruffle the feathers of his wing. She could see the misshapen areas of his fragile bones, and she almost gasped. Crow had told her that he couldn't fly, but he hadn't mentioned that it was this bad.

"The broken wings make it harder for you to change back?"

He nodded, his wing dragging on the floor.

"Come on then. Rest and shift in the morning." She sighed. No need to argue with him in this condition. "We're getting up

51

early so we can make it to the capital tomorrow."

Reva carried him to the mattress and set him on top of it. She then threw one of the blankets on the floor, and made a nest out of the material before placing him there. He closed his eyes as she backed away.

Removing her boots, Reva lay back on the lumpy mattress. As the rain started to pour, the scratching faded. But the cursed pixies would be out there until dawn, prowling around for prey.

She knew this because she'd once been the worst of them— a predator.

CHAPTER SEVEN

CROW

When the young Thelia left the Land of Oz, everyone had gone their separate ways. Lion holed himself up in the house the Wizard had gifted him, drinking himself into stupors and fighting whatever miscreant gave the slightest offense. Crow knew through observation that Lion was waiting for a worthy cause to swear his new-found courage to—if only Langwidere hadn't been the first one to make him an offer. Tin's decision to become one of Oz's personal guards had made less sense. The Tin Woodsman was skilled with an axe, but it hadn't been clear if he would be able to kill in defense of the Wizard, given he finally had a heart. Then his curse had returned. A terrifying thing, considering Crow's had been cured at the same time.

Crow, on the other hand, had only stayed in the Emerald City long enough to read every book there was on curses. Anything that could give him answers about Reva—his long-gone love. There was no bringing her back from the dead, but he'd wanted to know what happened for the sake of closure. The only useful bit of information he'd found was the existence of a red stone belonging to the Gnome King that could prevent a curse. A wonderful thing to know if he could get his hands on it for the future, but it hadn't answered his questions about Reva.

So, turning his attention away from the past, he'd traveled to the North and began his journey to find the human Dorothy Gale. It was a dreadful trip. Each step toward his former home felt heavier than the last, but it would be worth it if he found the girl his daughter had been swapped with.

In all the years between, he'd been to the capital only a handful of times. Each visit had been a little worse than the one before. Homes ransacked. Fae murdered. Cursed pixies haunting the night.

But now... Crow barely recognized the once-illustrious city.

More buildings were reduced to skeletons than were whole. Walls crumbling. Windows smashed. Roofs caving in. The yellow brick road gave way to emerald streets that had once glimmered in the sun. Now they were cracked, dented, and covered in so much filth that one would never know they were green. Death lingered in the air, decomposing fae with a hint of excrement. The buzz of danger rubbed against Crow's body.

"It's worse than I remember," he whispered to Reva.

She glared at him with wide, shocked eyes. "Worse than you remember?" she repeated in a strained voice. "The palace is little more than a pile of gemstone!"

Crow's gaze drifted to the iconic palace—missing peaks with holes in the walls large enough to see from this distance. The darkest black crept across the emerald stone like tainted veins. Whatever magic had once made it shine throughout the day and night had vanished, leaving it a dull, dingy green.

"Quit exaggerating. It's much bigger than a gemstone. However, it was whole the last time I was here—so, yes, worse." The palace had only been a little duller than before, thieves only struck at night, and the homes were in disrepair—not destroyed. But he hadn't been back in over two years.

Reva shook her head in disbelief. "I don't understand. I knew it would be bad here, but this? How did it happen?"

"As you know, Oz left—"

"Periodically, to make sure Ozma remained hidden in Loland, then he sent her to the dark place," Reva spat, eyes darkening. "And now he's abandoned the city all together."

"Apparently, yes." He cleared his throat as they navigated the muck-smeared streets. "The situation wasn't perfect before he left the city, however. The fae were growing tired of the Wizard ignoring them while he indulged his faerie fruit addiction. Work had been scarce and food low after a drought, so I believe a rebellion had been stirring. Which is likely why he'd suddenly thought to send Lion after Glinda. It would've left him virtually unopposed if he'd managed to take out all the territory leaders."

"It seems to have worked out quite well for him," Reva said in a low, sarcastic growl. "Ozma and I still don't know how he was able to get the silver slippers, though."

"A very good question," he agreed. "Maybe he's dead."

"He'd better not be dead—Ozma deserves the chance to show him *exactly* who he hid away all those years by ending his life with her own hands!" Reva scowled. "She never got to meet her father, Pastoria, and never will because of the Wizard."

Pastoria was the king before the Wizard murdered him and wasn't the brightest of fae. Crow wasn't sure if Ozma was capable of revenge. When she approached him outside the brothel, she'd seemed too sweet for such a bloody task, but then again, he didn't know her like Reva did.

After a few more streets, his stomach growled. He shielded his eyes and glared at the sky, trying to remember how long ago they'd eaten. The cursed pixies had chased them the night before, then he'd slept for hours in the nest Reva made until he woke to find her tossing and turning from a nightmare. And all through Reva's morning meal, he was still stuck in his bird form. She had offered to share the food, but his beak had healed from its break badly, just like the rest of him. While it looked fine, opening it wide enough to eat was too painful. They'd munched on fruit while they walked mid-morning, after he regained enough energy to transform back into a male, but he was more than ready for something more substantial.

"It's nearly midday," he said. "Would you like to find something to eat? I'm sure we could find a couple gremlins to skewer, or a redcap if you want something extra bloody."

"You're disgusting." Her nose wrinkled upward.

"This is the Emerald City. Fae eat fae because there's little else to go around."

"I'd rather starve."

Crow chuckled. "I was jesting." *Partially.* They did resort to eating each other on occasion, though he would also prefer starvation. "Are you absolutely sure there's a cure for my other form inside the palace?"

"When did I say I was sure? I said Oz would never destroy his potions." Her eyes slid over his body. "But if there's a way to fix your broken bird form, it will be somewhere in Oz's collection."

Crow swallowed hard. Reva appeared to hate him, but she'd still come with him for the *chance* of a cure. The question now was whether or not someone had ransacked the Wizard's private rooms. Odds might not be in their favor, but he didn't want to tell Reva that when she wasn't thrilled about coming into the Emerald City. Besides, she had to know that already.

"Forget about eating," Reva announced. "We're going straight for the potions and getting the fuck out of here."

A scream came from somewhere in the distance and Crow suppressed a shudder. He was in no mood for a fight, preferring this to be a stealth mission instead. Get in, get the cure, get out. Groups of fae lingered in the streets with swords and bows and spears. Their suspicious gazes followed Crow and Reva everywhere they went.

A feather-light touch brushed across Crow's side, and he leapt away from it, straight into Reva. A male sprite snickered, his spindly fingers wrapping around the ropes hanging from

Crow's neck. "Spare some rope?" he asked, flashing pointed black teeth without a whiff of shame.

"The fuck?" Reva hissed.

"No, actually." Crow attempted to pry his clothing from the would-be thief's death grip.

"Just a little?" he whined. "It doesn't take much to hang a nixie."

Crow let his blades drop. The sprite's eyes darted down to the gleaming metal and his smile froze. A nervous chuckle escaped his throat before he released the ropes and fled. "It could've been worse," Crow mused to Reva once the thief was out of sight.

"Let's not find out."

After that, they began walking a little faster and were soon at the perimeter of the palace. Groups of scarred, battle-ready fae gathered around small blazing fires, despite the sun shining brightly overhead. The kindling appeared to be broken planks from homes with odds and ends tossed in for good measure. A child's toy frog and a wooden portrait frame smoldered in a heap of embers, and flames still licked up the side of a broken mantel clock in another. There were mounds of dirty, blood-stained clothes, both adult and child, with an even larger pile of footwear nearby. Wooden crates formed a perimeter between them and the hardened fae and, past them, another row of crates ran in front of haggard-looking palace guards covered in grime.

"What's all this?" Reva whispered to Crow.

Crow nodded toward a painted sign that read *Onyx City*. It was appropriately named, visually and metaphorically. The heart of Oz was rotten—it was no wonder the rest of the territories followed. Crow's gaze traveled up the palace walls just a few yards away. The black lines seemed to pulse as if the building had a heartbeat. "They seem to have created their own headquarters," he said quietly.

"Not from around here, are you?" a male called from the nearest fire. The hobgoblin was larger than most at nearly five feet with black burn scars covering the left side of his face and neck. He wore layers and layers of clothing as if he were afraid someone would steal them otherwise. Given the piles of clothes, maybe that wasn't such a longshot. "There's no getting into the palace. Oz abandoned us, but Pastoria's magic is still strong as ever. Unless you can bribe a guard into letting you loot the place, no one goes in."

"And no one comes out," another fae, this one a leprechaun with wooden teeth, added dramatically. "We're the authority here now, if you want to petition us. 'Course you'll need vouchers for food and shoes and the like."

Crow and Reva meant no harm within the palace, but taking a potion could be considered thieving. The magic barrier could very well bar them entry unless there was a sanctioned escort. The guards looked utterly miserable at their posts, not that Crow could blame them. Who did they serve now that Oz was gone? Who paid their wages? Were taxes even making it to the palace? It was a miracle they hadn't abandoned their positions and let Pastoria's magic do their jobs for them.

"Not today," Reva told the leprechaun. Then she grabbed the ropes around Crow's neck and practically dragged him away from the surly fae.

"What's the matter?" Crow asked when they were out of earshot. Then, when his back hit the cool wall of a former eatery, the memory surfaced of her holding his bird form near her breast until they were safely inside the stone home. It wasn't like this the night before. Then it had been a matter of life and death, but now it felt more intimate. He lifted his brows suggestively. "Or could you not keep your hands off me another moment? Like last night."

"When I saved your life from the cursed pixies?" Reva *tsked* and quickly yanked her hand back from where it still gripped the rope near his neck. "You need to get us inside."

Crow chuckled without meaning to. "I'm open to ideas, my love."

"You're *Crow*. The fae who helped the savior of Oz kill ... well, *me*. Are you going to pretend you don't have some level of notoriety? That there isn't a single guard who would escort us inside and take us exactly where we need to go?"

Crow opened and shut his mouth. She was right, of course, but he loathed using his status for favors. It always felt to him as if he hadn't done much of anything to help young Thelia. Sure, he'd protected her along the yellow brick road and rushed to save her from... He glanced at Reva and chewed his bottom lip. But that was something anyone would do, especially a father, even if he hadn't realized it until after the fact. There were exceptions to not asking for help, though, and he needed his bird form fixed.

"Won't you be jealous, seeing them fawn all over me?" he asked.

"I see you're starting to act like your old self again. Please don't." Reva rolled her eyes, groaning, and marched back to the palace.

He was feeling like his old self too. Reva brought that out in him, and he most certainly *would*. Too many days had been wasted focusing on earning Reva's forgiveness instead of saving Oz. Especially when one would lead to the other.

The fae of Onyx City all watched them return with wary expressions until Reva leapt effortlessly over a crate. The self-imposed rulers descended then—golems, bodachs, hags, and a dozen other species. Crow easily hopped over the barrier and released his blades.

"I don't need you to save me," Reva shouted over the sudden shriek of enemies.

Crow gave her a quick smirk before slicing out at a ghoul with his blades. Ruby blood sprayed from the wound on the fae's chest. A warm mist sprinkled Crow's face. "Maybe I want you to save me."

"You're assuming I'd bother," she yelled as lightning crackled along her fingertips.

A bright flash of green slammed into the hoard, knocking

them backward. A slight prickle of Reva's energy struck him—a small jolt she must've given him on purpose. She had too much control for it to be an accident. Crow shot her a surprised look before throwing his head back with a laugh.

"Move before they get up," Reva demanded.

Crow followed her over the second barrier, where the elves on either side of the palace gates lowered into a fighting stance. "Good day," Crow called before they approached. "Lovely weather we're having."

They didn't react, their faces expressionless.

Crow sighed inwardly. This wouldn't work if they'd become someone's puppet—doubly so if there was someone within, ruling Oz quietly. "Any chance we could get inside? As a personal favor."

The two elves exchanged a quick glance and recognition lit their faces. "Crow?" the white-haired one asked. "You're … Crow, aren't you?"

"At your service," he answered with a flourishing bow.

The guards shifted nervously before the taller one spoke. "The Wizard isn't available for visitors."

"Oh, please. Who do you think you're kidding?" Reva growled. "I spent the last decade in another world and even *I* know he ran off."

At the mention of the dark place, Crow tilted his head to study her, to glean even the smallest hint of what it had been like there. But Reva gave no outward clue about what she'd lived through.

"Who are you?" the second guard asked.

"She's helping me," Crow answered before Reva could reveal her identity. Cursed or not, she had devastated countless families during her time as the Wicked Witch of the West. She needed to defeat Locasta before anyone discovered who she was. "We've just come from ending Langwidere's reign and are in need of a healing potion."

He felt Reva's angry stare on the back of his head, though he wasn't sure if it was because he hid her name from them or because he took credit for Thelia's kill. But the new victory might convince them that he was trying to help Oz yet again. They could clear up the misunderstanding later.

"Langwidere is dead?" the one with white hair asked, violet eyes bright with excitement. "The South is free?" When Crow nodded, the guard sheathed his sword. "I... I can send my family home," he whispered to his friend. "Our oaths prevent desertion, but our families can leave. It has to be safer for them in the South than it is here if Langwidere isn't there to steal their heads." Then, to Crow, "What of Glinda? Have you seen her?"

Crow hesitated. The Southern fae adored Glinda and telling the guard that she was dead wouldn't earn them any favors. Yet, he couldn't lie. "Glinda fell to Langwidere," he whispered with sincere compassion.

Shocked silence followed before the taller male cleared his throat. "You just need a potion?"

"That's all," Crow assured him.

He nodded. "Take them to Oz's chambers. I'll keep watch here."

"This way," the white-haired fae beckoned eagerly. "I'm Avo, by the way."

"Nice to meet you, Avo," Crow said with a smile. Then he winked over his shoulder at Reva, receiving an eyeroll in return.

Inside, debris covered the once-illustrious courtyard. Large chunks of emerald were pushed along the palace walls in an attempt to keep the area clean, but small pebbles and powdered gemstone were ground into the bricks. The high arched windows were either smashed, revealing makeshift curtains hung inside, or webbed with cracks. Each stair leading up to the crooked main doors shifted beneath their feet, and the deep, earthy scent of the fires gave way to that of mold and decaying sea life.

Avo led the way through the deathly-quiet palace and began up a long, winding staircase. Patches of walls were ten shades darker where portraits had hung. The throw rugs, once vivid and plush, were halfway gone from what looked to be rabid wolves chewing on them. Vases appeared to have imploded where they sat, a shower of glass flowing out around their intact bases. Worn chairs were scattered in random places—in hallways and corners and stacked on top of each other. Overhead, broken chandeliers swayed on thinning ropes.

"There's a bit of a phouka infestation," Avo informed them as they climbed higher and higher. "But most of the guards broke their oaths and took off shortly after Oz left. We tried to open the palace to the citizens of the Emerald City at first, but none could make it through Pastoria's barrier."

"That says a lot," Crow mused.

"It does," Avo agreed, looking back at Crow and Reva every few steps. "The Oz you helped create was the true golden age for us. You aided Dorothy when she saved our world and rid us of the Wicked Witch."

Crow winced, but said nothing, though he desperately wanted to defend Reva. He knew she was most likely seething behind him.

"Everyone talks about how kind you are, both before the Wizard broke your curse and after. Always willing to help, they say. And you're the smartest fae they've met. I heard you studied every curse in detail."

"It's better to know how to break a curse before it's cast," he said casually. There was no need to explain that he was hoping to understand exactly what Thelia had done to defeat Reva. There was also his own curse—the Curse of Unknowing—that he wanted to avoid ever experiencing again. At least that particular research had ended with him learning about an object from the Gnome King that could potentially deflect it. He just didn't have it in his hand.

"And avoid getting cursed again, I'm sure," Avo continued. "You were the only fae of the Golden Four not to relapse or let it destroy you. If you ask me, you're the real hero, besides Dorothy. You have brains, heart, *and* courage."

"Brains, heart, and courage, my ass," Reva mumbled angrily under her breath.

Crow twisted around to smirk. "It was teamwork," he told Avo, but patted his chest over his heart and pointed at Reva. "Speaking of Lion, he's dead too. And Tin's broken his curse for good this time. He helped us defeat Langwidere and Lion."

He purposely didn't mention Thelia's return, though he knew the rumors were already circulating. That was how he'd learned she'd been with Tin.

"It's really true?" Avo asked desperately. "Langwidere and Lion are dead? And the assassin isn't heartless anymore?"

"It's true," Crow promised.

Tears glistened in Avo's eyes. "You're going to save us again."

It wasn't a question, which made Crow uncomfortable. That was too much pressure to work under when he simply wanted to focus on avenging his family for the moment.

"Here it is," Avo said, pointing at a bright green door with a darker emerald stripe down its center. Peeling gold filigree framed it from the top of the wall to the bottom. "Oz's private chambers."

"Thank you." Crow gently squeezed Avo's shoulder and strode into the room.

A large glass case of potions stood directly across from him, beckoning him closer. He hurried to it and scanned the fading labels with hope building in his chest. There was an assortment of differently-shaped vials in a variety of colors. Some had pointed tops, others completely round, and a few curved designs. There were cures that bubbled, potions that swirled as if being stirred, and liquid that glimmered in the faint light of the room. A row of tin boxes sat on the bottom shelf with glass tops, showing pellets and tablets to be ingested.

"Try that one," Reva said, stepping up beside him. "It says *mending*."

Crow plucked up the blue vial from Oz's personal collection.

It could mean mending bones or mending literally anything else, especially with Oz being mortal. On occasion, he was known to call things by different names than the fae.

"Or this one." Reva lifted a brown vial reading *healing*.

"What do you think the difference is?" Crow asked, fingers nervously twitching. The realization that this could be dangerous slowly crept in. What if the potions crippled him further? Or, without knowing the proper dosage, killed him?

"This one says *bones*." Reva handed him a third bottle, this one clear with a tiny pebble resting at the bottom of the liquid.

Crow laughed without humor. "If you wanted to mutilate my body, there are easier ways to go about it."

"I'll keep that in mind if these don't do the trick."

Crow gently tucked the vials into his pack. "I'll have a healer look at them first."

"You say that like we have time," she said with an edge of annoyance.

"You say *that* like we have time to deal with my growing an extra limb."

"Your ability to shift isn't exactly useful," she snapped. "If it were, Locasta would've died the night she broke into our home."

Crow blanched. She wasn't wrong, but it stung more than her zap of lightning had. If he'd been stronger that night—had better magic—all their lives would've been different, so how could he be angry over the outburst? There wasn't a day that he didn't blame himself. "I'm sorry, Reva," he said quietly so Avo wouldn't hear her name. Most knew her as the Wicked Witch of the West, and even though no one had spoken her name after the curse, most still remembered it.

Some fleeting emotion appeared on her face. Regret? She opened her mouth to reply when a soft scratching sounded from inside the wardrobe beside the medicine cabinet.

"Shit," Avo called. "Hurry. That's the phouka!"

CHAPTER EIGHT

REVA

W hat the fuck were phouka doing inside the palace? There shouldn't be any of those blasted pests in the Emerald City— *Onyx City*—at all or anywhere near here. They belonged at the edge of the South near the Great Sandy Waste where they'd been banished.

Even though she missed Ozma's presence tremendously, Reva was relieved her friend wasn't here to try and combat these heinous beasts without her magic. Running or climbing away from them wouldn't be enough because they could fly. Nothing in the dark place had wings.

"Hurry!" Avo called as he whirled around and sprinted out of the Wizard's old room.

Reva clasped Crow by the elbow and tugged him out of the area.

Crow shot forward, and she followed him down the hallway, catching up with Avo.

"The phouka always rouse first before the night beasts come." Avo held his chest, breathing heavily. "We try to keep them out, but the sneaky bastards always find their way back in."

A buzzing picked up, joining the sound of clawing against the walls. Just as Reva turned, a swarm of ravenous creatures, with dark bloodred wings, blinding white eyes, large pointed ears, and brown fur covering their small bodies, barreled their way. Long tails curled behind them. Crow slammed the door, but she knew it wouldn't be enough to stop them.

Reva stood, prepared to destroy them with a single spark once they tore open the door, but her magic didn't ignite. She tried it again, waiting in vain for the thunder to rise. Lips parted, she stood stunned, unable to move, until she was lifted from the floor by Crow's strong arms.

"Why aren't you running?" Crow shouted as he set her on the floor. She didn't hesitate as she sprinted down the spiral staircase, its green gemstones flickering. The sound of the door being thrown against the wall echoed from above them.

As they reached the bottom, Avo swung open the front entrance and hurried behind the door. The swarm of phouka dodged down the staircase, screaming a high, distorted sound. Crow swiped at the air, blades extended. A creature with gnashing teeth came for him, and its blood sprayed as he ripped it to shreds with his blades. Reva rushed in his direction, knocking him to his back as the swarm flew over them at a quickening pace.

Reva waited to be torn to pieces. She continued to hover over Crow while trying to summon the lightning within her to life.

The sounds stopped. Everything stopped. The world around her had grown silent, just as her thoughts had. Magic surged within her before flickering out. The last ten years without magic had made her feel less than whole, and she didn't want to feel that again.

A loud bang came from behind her, and Reva turned her head over her shoulder to find Avo standing in front of the door that he'd slammed shut. Not a single phouka in sight.

"You saved my life," Crow said, and she knew he would have a smirk on his face.

She hurried to push her body away from his and stood, brushing off her jacket. "You saved mine first. The debt has been paid." If he hadn't picked her up, she would have still been standing at the door, frozen, attempting to use her magic.

Reva marched up to Avo. "Why is my magic not working? Where are the phouka headed?"

"They like to pick fights with the night beasts as soon as the sun sets. Langwidere unbanished them from the Great Sandy Waste to try and make this territory hers." His gaze flicked to her hands. "As for your magic, I can't say when it will come back. The Wizard's spells make it so that no one can do harm with their magic while inside the palace, but it's become unreliable lately with him gone. It will return at some point after you leave, but it won't be immediate."

Avo hadn't told them that earlier. She was about to use both her hands to do harm to his throat. Crow pulled her back before she could do it.

Unsheathing his sword, Avo put his opposite hand on the door handle. "I suggest going to Vronah's Tavern across the brick road, a few buildings down. You will still easily have access, Crow, but you will have to pull your companion through. The old magic there from Queen Lurline keeps it safe. She placed it there during the Wicked Witch's reign as a place to keep fae safe if needed, and it still holds to this day. If only all of the Emerald City could have had that magic… But as you see, the Land of Oz needs help. I would hurry before dark though."

Queen Lurline had become a victim to Langwidere sometime while Reva was the Wicked Witch. Reva was surprised Lurline's magic was still active, but at one point she had been a strong and powerful faerie. Lurline was Ozma's mother, but due to whatever spell Mombi or the Wizard cast, no one knew that particular truth.

The phouka belonged to Langwidere. That meant they were

now Thelia's. Once Reva defeated Locasta. Together, she and Thelia could help the Emerald City. Reva could try and break the curse of the night beasts while Thelia could call the phouka back to the Great Sandy Waste. If they didn't, the destruction would only continue, and she wouldn't allow that.

Outside, Reva couldn't see or hear the phouka. After Avo left them at the gates to gather with the other guards, Reva and Crow crossed over the Onyx City barriers and stepped onto the path.

As they made their way through the city, they passed a tailor shop where she used to have her dark clothing made, but it sat empty. Then a pastry wagon where Crow had once taken her as a surprise, now rested abandoned, wheels missing, paint faded. Finally, they approached Vronah's Tavern. The walls of the magical barrier glistened bright white, like specks of glitter. She wondered if Queen Lurline's magic would truly allow them entrance, but Crow didn't seem to share her concern.

Crow easily passed through the barrier, as though it already knew him. He held out his hand, and Reva hesitated for a moment before pressing her palm against the warmth of his so she could go inside. The rules of this barrier were unfamiliar to her, but she still thought that her tainted past could have prevented her passage. However, it didn't.

Her gaze met his light brown eyes, and a familiarity washed over her. She hurried and dropped his hand, moving toward the tavern. It was a large turquoise building covered in diagonal yellow stripes. Its black roof flickered with tiny white specks across the top like a night sky. Thick vines, with dark purple flowers blooming, covered the bottom portion.

Crow slipped past her, not saying a word as he opened the darkened glass door. He continued to hold it for her until she walked inside. She didn't know what she'd expected the interior of the tavern to look like. Perhaps for the place to be deserted. But it wasn't. A few fae lingered at rectangular tables, peppermint and vanilla filling the air. The fae laughed, drank, and kissed while low music from stringed instruments played. She wondered if these fae ever left the building or if this was just their way of life—to remain hidden.

It seemed like madness that fae had chosen to linger in the capital, regardless of this sanctuary. But for them, she supposed, the Emerald City was their home—one that would become more dangerous as the night descended.

Reva stared at a long counter filled with pies, vegetable stew, and mugs brimming with ale. From the magic she felt swirling around her, she knew food could easily be prepared and beverages served in a never-ending supply. Behind the counter, two female dryads gossiped to each other, their shoulders and breasts covered in tree bark. Their hair flowed a grassy green with twigs and white flowers entwined.

One's flaming orange irises flicked to Crow and her whole face lit up. "You're here! We were beginning to wonder if we'd see you again."

The other dryad bit her lip and smiled. "You've returned to save us again?"

Something ugly pulsed through Reva's veins and none of it was her magic.

"Sauli! Milla! I've missed seeing your faces." Crow sauntered forward and winked at the dryads, scooping up a cup of ale. "The South and West have been reclaimed, and Langwidere and Lion are dead. My companion and I hope to liberate the rest of Oz next." He handed Reva the mug, shooting her a wink as well.

Reva rolled her gaze to the silver ceiling where yellow bubbles floated along the top. Taking a sip of the ale, then downing the rest, she walked away from the conversation and sat at a table in the corner with no other occupants nearby. Above her hung a portrait of a young Oz. His dark hair was swept behind his mortal ears and he wore a pathetic maroon suit from his world. A red, bloody mark had been drawn across his throat. She wanted to slash his real flesh herself.

"They gave us room 22 upstairs," Crow said, interrupting her thoughts. He placed a steaming bowl of stew in front of her along with the key.

Carrots and potatoes slowly spun within the liquid as she stared at it. "That's fine." She sighed, glancing over his shoulder at the dryads who were still batting their eyelashes at Crow's turned back. "Take the potions now."

Reva stuck the key into her pants pocket while Crow took out the three vials.

"Maybe I should drink them one at a time and give it a few hours."

"Just take them, Crow." Her nails rapped impatiently on the table.

He chewed his bottom lip as he set the vials on the table between them. "I might have to be in my other form for them to work."

"Fucking drink them already." In all honesty, Reva didn't want to have to see his other broken form again. The thought made her stomach sink.

Crow grimaced but drank each one until they were empty.

"Do you feel any different?"

"Patience, my love." He flexed his hands as if testing them. "Do you know how many concoctions Oz made trying to become immortal? Who knows? Maybe he is now."

The possibility that Oz would never die unnerved her. "That wasn't my question."

"Nothing feels different yet."

Several worn books were stacked atop the table beside them. Crow reached across, plucked up the top tome, and cracked it open. She furrowed her brow as she watched his eyes shift back and forth across each line. Always reading. Even before his curse.

The night before, he hadn't known she'd woken in the morning before he had. He hadn't known that she'd had nightmares of the dark place, but not only that... She'd had a dream of him in his male form, touching her, tasting her. It had jolted her in a nostalgic way and caused her to have to face the other direction, sleepless. And he didn't need to know either.

Unable to study him anymore, she stood with her stew and walked to the opposite side of the room, past a table of raven-maids, their faces and arms decorated in feathers, their drunken singing followed by high-pitched laughter.

She continued to the back of the room where a bookshelf painted to look like tree bark took up the entire area. Reva started reading the titles as she ate her stew, the spices purely delectable—she didn't realize how much she'd missed their rich taste while trapped in the dark place. As for reading, it wasn't something she enjoyed. It had always been something she had to do. An endless chore. She could never enjoy stories, only ones that involved history.

"You look like you could use a bit of relief for the night," a deep male voice rasped.

She turned toward a tall fae male, not unattractive. But she preferred darker hair. His auburn locks were braided along the sides of his face and the rest flowed behind his back. Reva was about to turn around and walk away when she thought about the female dryads behind the counter. Crow had never answered her question from the day before. How many legs had he spread apart while she'd been away? Had he been inside one—or both—of the dryads?

Her fists tightened, her magic still gone. Reva wanted to forget, wanted to relieve herself. She set her bowl down on the shelf and fished out the key from her pocket. "My room?"

"She's mine," Crow rumbled beside her before the male could issue a response.

The auburn-haired male looked as though he was going to tell the new guest to fuck off, until his eyes widened in recognition. "Crow. You're back."

Crow rubbed his knuckles as though he wanted to extend those hidden blades of his. "For the night."

The male cast a glance between Crow and Reva, then cleared

his throat. "Hope to see you soon." He turned and walked to the counter where the two dryads were now focused on the auburn-haired fae.

Reva clenched her jaw, chest heaving, and turned toward the sparkling emerald staircase in the corner. She left Crow standing there and marched up the steps. Only he didn't remain. His booted feet thumped against the planks, a minimal distance behind her.

At the top, the hall branched off in several directions. Lanterns lit up the walls with light pink flames. In between each lantern hung a letter—*N. E. S. W.*—representing the first letter of the different territories.

After she found door 22 in the Eastern wing, Reva pushed the key in and unlocked it with a soft click. She opened the entrance and stepped inside. Before she could shut the door, Crow's hand closed around the edge of the wood, preventing it from latching. She should have known he wouldn't simply sleep out in the hallway like he had at Glinda's. She could hear the frustration in his rasping breaths.

Reva stepped back, allowing him access into the room, then slammed the door and backed him up against a striped wall. "I can fuck whomever I choose."

Crow inhaled sharply and scowled. "You would've regretted it."

"And you don't think I'd regret fucking you?" she asked, incredulous.

"Not when I know what you don't like." He leaned forward and whispered near her ear, his warm breath caressing her neck. "What you *do* like."

Reva couldn't stop her traitorous body from heating at the words and reacting to his nearness. But then all she could see was Thelia being ripped away, the victims she'd killed in her monstrous form, and being alone in that dark place.

She leaned forward, close, closer, pressing her lips right beside his ear, stroking the curved point with her tongue. "And

I know *exactly* what you like. My hand pressed in the folds of your ass, my tongue at the head of your cock. After that, you inside me, while I lick and nip at the spot right behind your ear." Gliding a finger gently down to the area, she pushed his dark hair out of the way. "Me on top of you, taking control, then you behind me to finish." As she drew even nearer, her body flushed with his, she could feel him hardening against her stomach. She smiled bitterly. "But alas, it's not happening."

Whirling around, she sauntered to the edge of the bed and sank down, realizing she'd not only done a disservice to him, but to herself as well. She refused to let it show.

Crow remained against the wall, chest heaving.

"We need to go to the Gnome King before we continue north," Crow finally said.

"Why?" She didn't like how he so easily changed the topic when her body still felt on edge. "And now you want to suddenly take a second detour? You failed to mention this earlier. No."

"He has a red stone that can prevent Locasta from changing us into something else. I tried to find it several times before and couldn't. So, as of now, it's only hearsay but would be worth the risk. She'll be too dangerous for us without it."

Reva understood what he was saying but all she heard was Locasta, Locasta, Locasta. Even hearing the bitch's name from his lips angered her. "Why don't you just go back to being Locasta's whore?" And that was the first time she'd truly regretted something she'd said to him thus far. Because she remembered the stories he'd told her of how the Northern Witch had treated him.

Pushing off from the wall, he moved toward her, deadly silent. He pressed his fists on the mattress on either side of her legs, his nose almost touching hers. "You want to know who I've fucked for the last twenty-one years? No one. There's only ever been you—my *wife*—on my mind. So stop treating me unfairly. Even if we both think I deserve it." His eyes glistened with anger as they burned into hers.

Reva was at a complete loss for words. She'd assumed, with him thinking she was dead, that he would have moved on. Even after everything *she'd* done to him, to Thelia, to the Land of Oz, he still hadn't touched another. *Wife*. She'd married him. Loved him. But now she wanted to pretend it had never happened, not truly because of what he had done but what *she'd* done.

Her words were frozen in her throat as he backed away and turned for the door. He was going to leave her here. Alone. And it wasn't something she really wanted. Not again.

"Wait! Don't go!"

Clenching his teeth, Crow glanced over his shoulder. "I'm only going downstairs to get you an apple." He opened the door and softly shut it, despite the anger still rippling off him.

Outside her window, the sounds of the night beasts began to rouse, growing louder and louder, but not any louder than her thoughts.

Reva had been awful to Crow and he was still going downstairs to get her a damn apple. Hot tears ran down her cheeks, and she remembered why she'd chosen to stay angry. Because this, this emotion, this *caring* hurt more than anything.

She leapt from the bed and threw the curtains closed, attempting to shut out the sounds from the night beasts as well as her thoughts.

CHAPTER NINE

CROW

The woven chair rocked unevenly when Crow plopped himself into it. His elbows went directly to the glossy wood bar top, and he hung his head in his hands. Reva's anger was understandable but to pretend they weren't married? It was a secret to everyone except them and Whispa, but that didn't mean it wasn't true.

"Rough journey?" Milla, one of the dryads, asked. Her deep brown skin was covered in pieces of mossy tree bark and green leaves were nestled in her carefully bound hair. Her friend, Sauli, from earlier was gone now, as were most of the other customers.

"You could say that."

Reva had taunted him so cruelly … then asked him not to go. Had she asked only because she'd been full of lust? The way he'd leaned in, close enough to kiss her, was so reminiscent of their first time sleeping together. She'd had a lash in her eye back then and he was trying to help get it out. Instead, the sexual tension snapped, and it had only taken seconds for their clothes to hit the floor. They'd fucked in front of the fireplace in her palace for hours. But tonight, Reva had tried to take a *different* male to their room. Crow loved her … he didn't want that to be how things were between them.

Crow lifted his head, ignoring the pain in his chest, and forced a smile so the dryad wouldn't pry into his current problems as any bar keep might. "It's good to see you again, Milla."

Milla's large eyes gleamed as she set a large, foaming mug down in front of him. "I wasn't sure you would remember me. It's been how long? Seven years? Eight?"

"Something like that," he agreed, regretting that he hadn't stopped in on his last visit to the city. The mead drew his attention with beads of condensation rolling down the glass. He shouldn't—clouding his mind was at the very bottom of his list—but his muscles were so tense. Perhaps just one drink to relax himself...

"It sounds like you've been busy, though. Ridding us of Langwidere and now you're heading north to face Locasta. The Land of Oz will never be able to repay you."

"The room and drink will suffice." Crow wiped the foam from his mouth and stared into his now-empty mug. Milla set another in front of him without missing a beat. "Besides, there are no guarantees that Locasta won't kill us instead."

Milla shook her head. "Don't underestimate yourself, Crow. You helped Dorothy all those years ago and now—"

"Now," Crow interrupted, "I have to find the Gnome King and convince him to give me something extremely precious and irreplaceable. What are the odds he'll be feeling generous?"

"Slim to none," Milla said stoically.

Another full mug found its way into Crow's hands. "I tried getting it from him a couple times. Without asking for it, obviously. Stealing it was much easier—or so I thought. It turns out that the Gnome King excels in setting traps."

The dryad winced. "I've lost a few friends to their nets. If the gnomes don't eat their catch, they use them to mine stone … then eat them later."

Crow finished his third mug of mead in a large gulp and sighed. His mind was a little fuzzy around the edges and he still had to figure out how to get out of the tavern without Reva following. There was no way he was taking her to the Gnome King's doorstep. He wasn't even sure why he'd mentioned it to her. "I need to go get some sleep," he mumbled. "Any chance you have an apple before I head back upstairs?"

"We do." Milla studied him for a moment. "You still look a bit wound up though. Would you like me to cut the apple up and sprinkle a sleep aid on it? It's completely harmless, but will give you a few hours rest, at least."

Crow opened his mouth to reject the offer, but then an idea struck. An awful, horrible idea that he knew he had no right entertaining. "That would actually be wonderful. Thank you, Milla."

By the time Crow returned to room 22, Reva was asleep on the far edge of the mattress. He set her sliced apple on the bedside table, the bruised pieces purposely missing. Not that he should care whether it was up to her standards, but that could've been due to the three large mugs of mead he'd downed as if they were nothing.

The drinks were, admittedly, a horrible decision. He felt no better about the fight with Reva, nor did it alleviate any of his guilt about the past. There was also the fact that he had to leave this sanctuary and find the Gnome King *without* Reva. The king had always been deviant—enslaving lesser fae in his mines, torturing his own subjects, raiding villages for gold, gems, and females—but ever since his queen was cut down by marauders, he'd killed any female who dared approach him. Locasta could simply curse them both again without the Gnome King's stone, though, so it was necessary for their victory. Crow worried about what he might need to trade the tyrant to get him to lend them the stone, but if it helped the Land of Oz and assured Reva her revenge, it was worth the price.

Crow eased himself onto the empty side of the bed, tucked an arm beneath his cheek, and watched Reva sleep. He wanted to reach out and stroke her cheek. Press his lips to hers. To *feel* her again. He wouldn't—not if she didn't invite him to—but that didn't keep his cock from stiffening.

Fucking mead. It had gone straight to his head. He knew he should still be frustrated with Reva.

"Did it work?" Reva mumbled without opening her eyes.

Crow jerked at the sound of her voice. Had she been awake the entire time? "Did what work?" he asked softly.

Her eyes cracked open, the slight glaze telling him she *had* been asleep. Or … Crow squinted. They were slightly puffy. Had she been crying?

"The potions," she clarified before he could question it further.

Crow rolled to his back to stare at the ceiling. "There's only one way to find out."

"Shift then," she said.

"Will you hold me close all night if I'm still broken? You know, to ease my disappointment." *Damn.* Definitely too much mead.

Reva groaned. "Perhaps I'll throw you out the window just to make sure you're not faking it." Something in her voice told him she wasn't serious.

Crow chuckled, but he wasn't about to call her bluff. He regretted downing all the potions at once slightly less than pounding drinks downstairs. If he needed to take them while in his bird form to work, their entire journey into the Emerald City was for nothing. He wasn't brave enough yet to find out the answer. Besides, if he shifted now—an extremely painful process given his shattered body—he wouldn't be able to shift back in time to leave Reva behind.

"Maybe tomorrow," he said to humor her. "Then you can

carry me again while I get in a nap."

"You're insufferable."

"I do try my best." He rolled onto his side, suddenly thoughtful. "If I asked you to stay here while I retrieved the Gnome King's stone, would you?"

Reva scowled, lifting one eyebrow as if to say *are you serious?*

He sighed. "I didn't think so. You are aware he kills every female he sees, yes?"

"And?"

"And, you're a female," Crow said, catching himself before adding *without power.* Her magic could return at any moment, but it didn't matter. Bringing her along wouldn't be wise.

Reva rolled her eyes. "We don't need his stone, Crow. Besides, you have no idea if it really exists, and even if it does, he won't just hand it to you. It would be more expedient to ambush Locasta without giving her the chance to curse us again."

Crow chewed his bottom lip. More expedient, yes, but he was less concerned with the speed of this mission and more so with their success. When he'd researched curses, a few books mentioned possible ways to avoid the Curse of Unknowing, but none were full-proof. The red stone belonging to the Gnome King was their best chance. All Crow knew was that he couldn't go through being cursed again. Not the forgetting and certainly not losing Reva. Thelia needed them, as well. They couldn't let their daughter suffer again.

"Reva?" he breathed. "Do you remember the last pub we spent the night in?"

"Not another word," she whispered without looking at him.

"Why not?" he asked. It was the same weekend Thelia had been conceived. "It happened, regardless of how you feel now."

Reva looked startled for a moment, and Crow couldn't understand why. But then her expression changed as she pushed up onto her elbows to peer down at him. "Whatever happened between us over twenty years ago happened to two different people. We are no longer them ... nor do I wish to be."

Crow's lips lifted in a wistful smile. "Like it or not, my love, you're still my wife."

Reva pursed her lips, her cheeks and neck growing splotchy. Crow knew she didn't say anything because there was no arguing that he was right.

"I'm going back downstairs to read for a bit." He took the plate of apple slices from the small table and handed them to her. "You should eat this before it turns brown."

"The dark place I was sent to... I was alone. For years. Hunted incessantly. The constant running and hiding without magic was unbearable. I'd never felt so vulnerable. Not until Ozma arrived. You weren't there, Crow. You weren't there..." Her last word came out as a whisper.

Crow balled his hands into fists to keep from reaching out to her. Once again, Reva had been in danger and he hadn't been able to do a damn thing about it. "I'm sorry."

Reva turned away from him and bit into a slice of the apple. Swallowing hard, Crow slipped from the room. Instead of returning to the pub where a few fae still congregated, he slid down the wall beside the door, resting his elbows on his knees, and tipped his head back. "Until death," he whispered the final line of their vows to himself.

The full moon lit the clearing. Stones lined the circular area around Crow, Reva, and their friend, Whispa. The pixie smiled as she led the wedding ceremony, calling on the spirits of the forest to bless the union. Reva had never looked more beautiful. She wore a soft black dress with sheer sleeves and strips of leather crossing over her swollen belly while Crow had donned a simple black tunic. Whispa carefully tied Crow and Reva's forearms together with a green ribbon, signifying life. Once Whispa spoke, Crow's eyes locked with Reva's and they barely blinked as the pixie asked them to repeat her words.

They would seek to make each other happy.
They would be each other's confidant.
Honor. Respect. Love.
They would champion each other.

Until death.

Crow's heart exploded with joy when Whispa untied the ribbon from their arms, signaling their wedding was at an end. There were no witnesses, save the pixie—it was too dangerous with Locasta searching all of Oz for them—but one day, they hoped to repeat their vows in front of everyone they loved—including the child growing in Reva's womb. Until then, Crow would cherish his new bride in secret.

Crow shook himself back to the present. The phantom taste of Reva's lips remained, and he rubbed at the ache in his chest. Reliving those memories only tortured him, so why did he allow his mind to wander there?

Heavy footsteps started up the stairs and Crow stood. It should've been long enough for Reva to finish her apple slices— and the tasteless sleep crystals Milla had sprinkled over them— so he re-entered the room to avoid making small talk with whoever approached. The plate was indeed empty on the table and Reva was curled in a ball in the center of the bed, fast asleep.

"I'm sorry," Crow said as he approached. He bent to pull a thick rope from his pack. "I'd say you would hate me for this, but you already do." He tied one of the most complicated knots he knew around one bed post, then moved to the next. "What's one more strike against me? Especially when it's something as small as this?"

Crow frowned at his own words. In comparison to endangering her life, it was a minor offense to tie his wife to the bed and temporarily abandon her. It was still a completely underhanded move though.

"I'm doing this to save your life," he added as if that made everything all right. She was going to kill him for this, regardless of his motives, and he couldn't blame her.

Once each corner of the bed had a tight knot, he carefully stretched each of her limbs and tied the other end of the rope to her wrists and ankles. Reva had always found his knots hard to untie. She'd nearly chopped down her favorite tree because his hammock was blocking her garden's sunlight and the knots were impossible.

The fact that he was hiding her boots in the wardrobe behind the extra blankets only added insult to injury. Crow knew Reva would escape her bindings quickly—whether it was because her magic had finally returned or because she screamed for help, was yet to be seen. When she did, having her search for her footwear would buy him a little extra time to finish his business with the Gnome King before she caught up.

He shouldered his pack, but hesitated. There was a chance Reva would simply continue her plan to take on Locasta without him. She had never wanted to travel with him in the first place, and she'd been very clear about the Gnome King being a waste of time.

Fuck. This was a bad idea.

She would just have to get over it.

Or not.

But she would be alive and Locasta would be dead.

"Sleep well," Crow told Reva, and left her there, her face perfectly serene. He knew that the next time he saw her, the expression she wore would be far from peaceful.

CHAPTER TEN

REVA

*T*he Western Witch moved lithely behind a tree as four sets of steps came closer. Three fae males and the pathetic human child. Even though the slippers weren't on the Wicked Witch's feet just yet, she could feel the thrum of the shoes' magic pulse inside her, as though they were calling to her. Once the slippers were on her feet, no one would ever be able to stop her. Not even the one controlling her—Locasta. She didn't want to be controlled anymore—she wanted to rage all on her own, then rule the entire world.

Closer and closer the interlopers inched. The girl wore her hair in braids, and the clothing draping her was disheveled and hideous. One male with silver hair held an axe and was still a youngling, not quite into adulthood yet. Another's golden hair shone beneath the sun, his tail twitching behind him, his gaze frantically shifting in all directions. He was even more pathetic than the other two. Out from behind the shadow of the girl came another, his black hair sprinkled with feathers, dirt covering his flesh. The Witch's gaze fell to his stomach, where a ropy torn tunic showed his glistening skin proudly. Something pulsed through her. A sense of wanting to lick that skin, touch him, taste him. Absorb his heat from the inside out. Unwind his intestines and discover their flavor. She'd never felt such an intense wanting of someone *to die and become her meal.*

"How far do you think we are from the Emerald City?" the girl asked.

"It could be this way," the feather-haired fae said. "Or this way, or this way, or this way, or this way—"

"It's this way," the one holding the axe replied, rolling his eyes.

The Witch smiled. They were now coming directly toward her, and her winged minions sat above her in the trees, waiting for her to give them the signal to attack.

Closing her eyes, the Witch let the magic stir within her. A thunderous boom from her lightning came, and a growing emerald fire lit in the center of her palm. She threw the flame at the golden fae. He screamed and dropped to the ground, cradling his legs to his chest. The other two protectively placed the girl behind them, all while a strange animal yapped and yapped.

But the fire spread and spread around the Witch and her prey as she stepped out from behind the tree, drifting closer. The flames looped around them in a wide circle. She was going to kill them all. Her life had been built on destruction and chaos and she wanted them dead. The small, furry creature continued its defensive sounds, grating on the Witch's ears. She was the Wicked Witch of the West and she wanted to destroy, destroy, destroy.

"You're her. The Wicked Witch of the West," the girl said, peeking her head around the silver-haired fae.

The Witch gave a shrill laugh, holding up her hand with another ball of flaming fire, calling to her minions. Out from the branches, the creatures rose, circling above them, screeching, howling, aching with hunger.

"You have nowhere to hide now," the Witch said, her eyes falling to the silver shoes. Their shine, their glisten, their sparkle. She needed them and couldn't take her eyes off the slippers as she lunged forward, ready to tear the girl apart and hand the bones to her beasts.

As she shot forward, the feather-haired male pushed the girl to the fae with the axe. He spun the girl around, protecting her. At any time, he could have come at the Witch with his axe, but he must have known that she could easily light them both on fire if she chose. She liked toying with her prey.

"I suppose she'll be last to be eaten instead of first."

The feather-haired male tilted his head, appearing to not truly see her, as if he were looking at nothing. Was he a halfwit? He continued to stare at her, stare and stare and stare and stare. Her anger rose. A sharp throb came at her ankle and she let out a yelp. The strange furry creature had bitten her! A hard shove came from the tailed fae, hitting her in the back.

Unable to hold her balance, the Witch fell to the dirt. Before the one with the axe could swing his weapon, her winged minions were upon them. But her prey was already running and running when she stood. Her circle of flames had burned out after she fell and lost hold on her magic. She threw a parting gift of flame that brushed the feather-haired fae's hand, but he didn't stop.

"You can't run forever! The shoes will be mine," the Witch screamed, lighting up again.

Reva jerked awake, her eyes wide, her voice coming out in a raspy shout. Something held her back from leaping out of the bed, the room, herself. Her wrists and ankles were bound with rope. She searched the room with desperation for Crow. He wasn't there. What if an enemy had taken him?

Reva's gaze drifted to her legs, then wrists, as she pulled, kicked, tugged, and ripped. None of the knots would loosen. She recognized those damn knots. *Crow.* She knew without a doubt that no enemy had done this to her—it had been *him*. Grogginess slowly started to seep its way into her as the high from her nightmare finally left. By the darkness through the slit of the curtains, and the night beasts' vicious noises, she could tell it wasn't yet close to dawn. Crow couldn't have gotten far yet.

All her guilt from the dream of him in her past vanished. And to think she'd felt *sorry* for how she'd treated him since her return—had told him about the dark place. She'd even been close to apologizing. Well, not anymore. The Gnome King may murder females, but that didn't mean he wouldn't torture the males until they prayed for death.

Reva's magic crackled inside her. Clenching her fists, chest heaving, she tried to release it, even a small spark to burn the bindings. She didn't have the fire like she'd had as the Wicked Witch, but lightning would have worked just as well. Relief washed over her as she felt her magic there, even though she couldn't tell when it would be at full strength.

With a hard thrust forward, Reva shook and rattled the entire head board, hoping to push the bed through the wall. "Open the door!" she screamed and raged as loud as she could. *Someone* would hear her.

After what felt like endless screaming, a rattle came as the door was unlocked and pushed open. It was one of the female dryads. Milla.

"Untie me," Reva demanded, still shaking the bed.

"I'm not supposed to," she said, her expression apologetic.

Reva narrowed her eyes. "What do you mean?"

"I gave Crow a sleeping aid, but I thought it was for him. Before he left, he said to make sure you stay here and remain safe."

The apple. The *apple*. The bastard had known there was something on her fruit to make her sleep. And he knew not to mess with her apples.

"Listen to me, and listen to me carefully," Reva said, low and dangerous. "You're going to untie these for me."

Milla shook her head.

"I can't tell you who I am, but just know I'm going to help Dorothy save the world." Reva hated using Thelia's name in that way, hated using her daughter to do this. Yet, Reva couldn't reveal that she'd been the Wicked Witch because the dryad would have not only left her there, but probably would have pushed a blade into her heart, too.

"I don't understand." The dryad took a step back, instead of closer, and crossed her arms. "That doesn't make me want to untie you. Dorothy can save the world with Crow like before."

Reva released a frustrated growl "Crow is Dorothy's father and I'm her mother. Dorothy isn't human—she's fae."

"Sure..." The dryad sighed, not believing her. Yet, she moved toward the rope. "But I think you should be able to choose for yourself what you want to do—not have someone choose for you, even if death is the result."

Reva was about to yell at the dryad to cut the ropes, but she was already using a jeweled blade from her hip to slash through the bindings.

Leaning forward, Reva rubbed at her wrists. "For that, when all this is over, I promise your position in the Emerald City will be great."

"Wouldn't that be wonderful?" The dryad watched her carefully as if Reva were drunk on wine or from the sleep aid, but no recognition set in.

Hopping from the bed, Reva reached for her boots. Her hand only grasped air. "Where *the fuck* are my boots?"

The dryad lowered herself to search under the bed. "Crow had no boots with him when he left, so they have to be in here somewhere."

Blood coursing with rage through her veins, Reva opened the drawers of the dresser then threw open the closet door. In the back, behind extra blankets, peeked black laces. He was dead. So dead. But first she had to save his sorry ass before the Gnome King tortured him. Reva tugged on her boots and hurried out the door.

"He didn't leave that long ago, so you should be able to catch up to him," the dryad called.

When Reva rushed down the steps, into the dimly lit pub area, it was mostly empty, aside from a couple sipping on mugs while another fae male, with violet scales, sketched in a yellowing notepad.

The cursed pixies were still making their sounds outside, and she could hear the fighting escalating between them and the phouka. Perhaps they would be too distracted to notice her.

Another thought shot through her—Crow had really left during this? Her anger turned to fear. What if he hadn't survived?

Reva took a deep breath and slowly opened the door, stepping into the cool darkness. The scent of fresh blood hit her, and she couldn't help but think about how much crimson had truly been spilled here since she'd been gone. The entirety of Oz could have possibly been painted in it by now.

As she approached the protective barrier, she wondered again if Whispa was still alive in the swarm of cursed pixies. What about Ozma? Was she safe and whole on her own journey?

When a faint orange sun lit the horizon, the screeching from the creatures lessened. It wasn't that the night beasts couldn't survive during the day—they could—but their bodies would be in constant burning pain. When Reva was the Wicked Witch, she hadn't cared, hadn't worried about listening to their tortured cries. She'd made them carry out her duties, her searches, and her attacks without allowing them sleep, all while their bodies writhed from the sun's burn.

Reva shuddered at the memory of their screams. But then she remembered their elated cries as they lapped, bit, and tore into the fresh bodies she'd killed. Sometimes she hadn't killed them first—sometimes she would let the beasts fill their stomachs while her victims were still alive.

Reva hadn't realized she was still standing frozen at the magic barrier when a shrill shriek sounded not too far from her. Would the fae of Oz truly forgive her when they discovered who she was? Would they fear her? Or would they remember Reva, who'd fiercely protected the West. Either way, she would try to earn their forgiveness by ridding them of Locasta.

Taking a deep swallow and pushing her shoulders back, Reva silently crossed through the barrier. As the sun lifted higher and higher, the swirling yellows, oranges, and reds falling upon her, she didn't follow the green road leading back to the yellow. Instead, she ran to the back of the crumbled building, across from the tavern, and passed through the trees. The noises from the creatures of the night faded, but the Emerald City wasn't completely silent.

What Crow didn't know was that there was a shortcut to the Gnome King, so she was going to catch up to her *husband* much sooner than he ever could have thought.

CHAPTER ELEVEN

CROW

The skeletal pixies swarmed the trees outside of the Emerald City, their shrieks piercing his ears, but Crow had been expecting that. He wore his mask low, the beak covering his face, his head bent, as he slunk through the shadows. If he had more time, he would transform to see if his bones were healed so he could fly over the forest. It would take too long to regain the energy to transform back if the potions failed, though—and that was *if* the magic-depleting effects from the palace had worn off. When he'd left her, Reva's power had yet to return.

Crow plastered himself against a large tree covered in moss and held his breath. The beasts above him shifted on their perches, their heads cocking back and forth as they listened for the slightest sound. When a phouka crashed far away from him, the pixies took to the skies with an ear-piercing shriek. Crow used the noise and distraction to bolt.

On and on he went through the woods just outside of the Emerald City—running, waiting, throwing the occasional rock to send the cursed pixies investigating away from his hiding spot—until the sun broke the horizon. The mead was finally out of his system, but exhaustion replaced it. His mind was foggy, his limbs heavy. The little sleep he'd gotten since leaving Glinda's palace was broken and fitful, which made walking all night tip him toward the edge.

"Damn," he muttered as he stumbled over his own feet. *Just a few minutes…* A small rest, and then he had to keep moving. Crow pushed aside a sheet of vine-like branches to lean against the tree trunk. Hidden inside the natural tent, he tugged his mask down over his eyes and fell asleep.

Crow gasped, his eyes flying open. He looked frantically around for a threat but found none. Sun filtered through the trees and birds chirped overhead. All was serene. Except for Crow. Ever since the Wheelers had cut him out of his hammock when he'd been traveling with Thelia and Tin, sleeping outside had become nerve-racking. The few days that he'd spent tracking Reva were practically sleepless. Shaking his head, Crow eased himself to his feet. His pack was still fastened to his back, so after stretching quickly, he stepped outside of the tree's shelter.

His feet flew out from under him, his back smacking against the packed ground with a *thwack*.

He twisted his head as he was flung high into the air, trying to figure out what the hell had just happened, and found himself in an iron net. The net cocooned him as it swayed from one of the higher branches. On instinct, his blades shot out from his bracers, but they would do no good against an iron net. He rocked the net, shifting his weight around, forcing it to swing in an attempt to loosen the trap, but it held fast. After another moment of confused panic, he let out a long, shaky breath.

"Shit," he muttered. Why were so many hunters suddenly setting traps? He'd gone years without finding himself in one. Crow leaned on his pack to lessen the exposure of iron on his skin, but his arms still burned fiercely.

Just as he found a comfortable position and began looking for any weaknesses in the net, footsteps crunched on the forest floor. Crow's claws shot out again. His body tensed, ready to fight the owner of the trap.

"Well, well, well," a familiar voice purred from below. "Isn't this ironic?"

Reva.

Crow's heart slammed against his ribs. How had she caught up with him so quickly? "Hello, my love," he called as innocently as he could manage. "Fancy meeting you here."

"Yeah," she snapped. "Fancy fucking that. Since you allowed me to eat food with a sleeping aid and *tied me to the bed.*"

"If I remember correctly, there was a time you would've enjoyed being tied," he said with a sly smile. It had only happened once, but Reva hadn't complained. In fact, it was quite the opposite.

She rubbed at her temples and mumbled too quietly for Crow to make out her string of words. When her eyes flicked back up to him, she said, "I have half a mind to leave you up there while I go get the stone by myself."

"Only half? Besides, I thought you didn't want the stone?"

Reva's lips turned up in a wicked smile. "I'll come back for you once I have the stone."

Crow chuckled to himself, but then she walked off. The amusement faded the farther she got, followed by a sweeping sense of disbelief. She was *actually* going to leave him there? "Reva," he called. "This isn't funny!"

Her faint laugh reached him from a few trees away. She was serious? *She was serious.* Crow shook the net, the iron burning his fingers. But he didn't care. No way was he letting his wife seek out the Gnome King alone—not when it was an instant death sentence. And *especially* not if the rumors were true about him fucking beautiful women first.

"Reva Etain Westbloom!" Crow shouted, using her true

name for the first time since he'd learned it. He'd wanted to use it so many times over the past few days to get her to listen to him but knew it was wrong. This was different.

Her footfalls immediately stopped.

"Get me out of this net right now!" he ordered.

Reva held a neutral expression as she crashed back through the forest to him and disappeared under the branches where Crow had just napped. A moment later, the net plummeted to the ground. Crow landed on his hip with a loud *thud*.

"As classy as ever," he said through the pain. "Reva Etain Westbloom, I release you from my control."

Reva flew out from between the hanging branches with fury swirling across her features. Her lips pulled back in a low growl as she ripped the net away from Crow. Her hands quickly curled into the strands of decorative ropes around his neck, and she twisted them until they nearly choked him. "You *dare* use my true name?"

"You left me little choice," he said earnestly. Though, he did regret calling it so loudly when there was no telling if other fae lingered nearby. "It's the *Gnome King*."

"Don't act like you're any safer going alone than I am. He would still torture you," she spat.

Crow pried Reva's hands from his ropes and stood, kicking away the net where it clung to his boots. "He would have to catch me first."

Reva looked pointedly at the net on the ground. "Clearly a manageable task."

"Untrue. I've snuck in a few times already without detection." Crow cocked an eyebrow. "Besides, you were in a net first, my love."

Reva *tsked*. "Consider us even. We're wasting daylight."

There was no arguing that point, and they resumed their travels in tense silence.

Creatures rustled in the brush, snorting, huffing, growling. It wasn't the ones that sounded disgruntled that they had to worry about, though. Between him and Reva, it would take a fae with critical thinking skills to pose a threat—unless they traveled in a large group or were massive in size, which they weren't.

The fresh, dewy scent of morning gave way when the sun reached high in the sky, and they decided to take a break at a riverbank. Reva snared a small boar and cooked it over a fire while Crow set his pack down at the edge of the water. He could see every pebble at the bottom of the river, and tiny blue fish swam leisurely with the current. The sun glinted off the surface and Crow's skin itched beneath the layers of sweat and dirt. He pulled his shirt over his head and glanced back at Reva to make sure she was still within sight. A small smile turned up his lips when he found her staring straight at him.

"Care to join me?" he asked, unbuckling his pants.

Reva rolled her eyes and turned back to the fire.

Crow took his time scrubbing himself in the crystal-clear river. The scent of roasting meat had him salivating as he drew himself out of the crisp water. He stepped onto the riverbank and slipped his pants back on.

"That looks good," Crow told her as he sat on a nearby log. His hair hung in wet locks around his bare shoulders and face, droplets of water clinging to the feathers.

"You're assuming I'll share."

She was obviously still angry that he'd tied her to the bed and used her true name, but he wouldn't lie and say he was sorry. Crow shrugged at her words and dug through his pack for the unblemished apple he'd snagged from the pub before he'd left. A preemptive apology snack.

Reva's eyes followed the fruit as he tossed it into the air and caught it. "Fine," she mumbled. "You can have some." He knew she wouldn't be able to deny the apple, just as he wouldn't have been able to deny her anything.

Crow gave her a knowing wink and handed her the fruit.

"It's not poisoned, is it?" She took the apple begrudgingly, giving it a whiff before setting it aside while she carved them each a piece of meat.

"Is your magic back?" he asked after swallowing his first bite.

Reva shook her head. "Can you shift yet?"

Crow chewed his meat instead of telling her he was too scared to try. It was tender, but the flavor a little too grassy, yet fulfilling, nonetheless.

"Really?" she said, seeming to understand his silence. "After all we went through to get the potions? *Try it.*"

"There's no need to be hasty," he mumbled.

Reva sighed, some of her anger deflating. "I know you're fearful, but we need to know. The Gnome King is dangerous for us both, and I'm still powerless. If you can shift, it would at least give us *something* to work with."

Crow nodded. She was right—they needed to know. That didn't make it any easier, especially when he had a gut feeling that the answer would be unsatisfying. Setting his lunch aside, Crow closed his eyes and mentally prodded at his magic. When nothing happened, he poked at it a little harder. The part of him that contained his magic was brimming with it, but it simply rested there instead of responding.

"Are you going to shift or not?" Reva asked quietly.

Crow's eyes opened wide. "I... I can't."

"I should have guessed this." Worry lines formed on Reva's forehead. "But with the potions being for general healing, I thought perhaps you could. One of us should have waited outside the Emerald City Palace—"

"It's not that," Crow interrupted. "The magic is still there—I can feel it. It just seems to be paralyzed."

Reva stared down at the apple, turning it so the glossy skin caught the sunlight. "I think mine is getting better," she offered. "It's more awake than it was."

Crow blinked. Once. Twice. "What's more awake?"

"My power," Reva said as if it were obvious.

"Right, right," Crow said quickly to cover his building fear. Had they just been talking about her power? What was her power anyway? He could … turn into something. Maybe? Crow's lungs screamed for more air, but each of his breaths were hard won. His heart spasmed rapidly. "Reva," he breathed. He grabbed his head in his hands, desperate to hold onto her name before it vanished from his mind like it had when Locasta cursed him. "Reva, Reva, Reva."

CHAPTER TWELVE

REVA

"Reva," Crow murmured again and again, as though his immortal life depended on it. Reva studied him, her brow furrowing as he sat staring at the yellow flowering bushes along the riverbank.

Taking a hard swallow, Reva's chest tightened and her throat locked up. She'd never seen him this way, expressionless.

"Are you all right?" she asked, kneeling in front of him.

His head jerked up, his bright brown eyes meeting hers, wild. "I'm fine. I was just thinking about something. Go get cleaned up before we leave."

Perhaps his cursed past was haunting him the way hers had in dreams, in her thoughts. Something in her didn't want to leave him sitting there, but she nodded and stood.

As she stepped over small patches of faeriefly eggs in patches of flowers near the riverbank, she realized all her anger about Crow using her true name had vanished. And she knew why it had. Because she would have done the same damn thing. If he'd been in the room after tying her to the bed, she would have used his name to release her too. He could have left her behind when she'd been stuck in the net, and if he had tried, she would have used it then as well.

They were the same—both stubborn, both yearning for the other. Reva shook her thoughts away, feeling lightheaded. Why was she thinking about yearning? Her focus was on killing Locasta, and that was all.

Reva stared out at the glistening pale-blue river. Without another word, she slipped off her muddy boots and removed her clothing. She wondered if Crow was sneaking glances at her like she had with him when he was bathing. His naked chest, his toned arms, the smoothness of his backside. It was almost impossible for him to look better than she remembered, but he did.

"Stop," Reva whispered to herself. But her body was growing weightless, and she couldn't keep herself from looking back at him.

He wasn't peering at her, though. Instead, Crow sat in the same position, counting something over and over on each of his fingertips.

Those fingers she wanted in her hair, on her body, cradling her breasts, between her legs. Everywhere and anywhere.

Something wasn't right, but she pushed the feeling away as she stepped into the river. The cold water sent a chill up her spine, and gooseflesh sprinkled across her skin as she washed away filth from the journey.

She'd never felt like this before. Not with this *need*. She tried to wash her memories away again without peering at Crow, the way she had attempted back at Glinda's palace. But they always lingered, no matter how far she tucked them. They always would.

She needed to make herself think about something else.

It would take several days to get to the Gnome King. If he had still lived just past the Deadly Desert in his stone palace, it would have taken longer. The journey would've been a challenge to cross the desert, when touching it turned anyone's flesh to sand.

Once the Gnome Queen was brutally murdered, the king had never returned to his stone palace. Instead he'd stayed on land centered in the outskirts between the North and the West, luring fae females in, only to kill them in the end.

Because they weren't his queen. No one would ever be.

The females would go to him, believing they could change him, believing they could be his queen, that they could be the one to make him *feel*. But someone made purely of stone, with a hardened heart like Tin had once had, could never truly feel.

Thelia had told her Tin's story late into the night before she'd left. Oh, Thelia! Oh, how Reva wanted to spin in circles with Thelia and braid her hair and laugh together and eat baked delights.

Reva's excitement grew, her body becoming restless as she gazed at the sun, wondering how close she could get before combusting. She reached her hand up as if to touch it. Perhaps she could fly to the sun and find out. No, no, because that would mean she could die.

Her insides were alive, lit up with energy, wanting to burst free. The water was no longer cold, but hot, as if it would scald her skin. Her body felt off balance, like she'd drunk too much ale. She hadn't had any. Or had she?

Stroking and slicing her way across the lake to get back to Crow—*her Crow*—Reva could discuss all the games they could play with Thelia now that she was back. But they were supposed to go somewhere today. Oh, well, there were much more important things to do.

She sang to herself as she tugged on her clothes, not caring that they clung to her wet skin. As she tried to slip on a boot, she tripped over her own feet, dropping it. "Fuck those boots. I can be barefoot like Ozma." Ozma... Reva shrugged.

Smiling, she whirled around to find Crow in the same spot, but his eyes were focused on her now. For a moment, her stomach sunk, losing all its giddiness. The cornfield. That was where they would arrive next—the place where he'd spent ten years of his life.

Bah. She'd been selfish. For Crow, it would be similar to her revisiting the dark place. Oh, how she wished he'd been there with her in that lonely place. They could have played games there too. And possibly braided each other's hair. She laughed out loud, giddy, covering her mouth.

Crow moved toward Reva, on all fours like a baby dragon, his eyes never leaving hers. She laughed and laughed and laughed until it turned into a high-pitched shriek that reminded her of something.

Something bad.

Very, very, bad. "Naughty Reva, don't you worry, you aren't wicked anymore," she sang to herself.

As she spun and spun, she finally came to a stop, finding Crow on his knees in front of her. She gasped and released a giggle. He grabbed her hand and pulled her down to where he was.

"Something's wrong with me," he said, breathing hard. "I think—I think my curse is coming back."

Reva looked around, the world spinning and spinning, like she'd just done, except this time it was reversed. There was no game, there could be no games—she was becoming a wicked fae once more. She peered down at her skin. Was it just her, or did it glisten green beneath the sun? But even if she did turn wicked, she could have Crow be wicked with her this time. Be bad together. *No!*

This wasn't the curse—her body wasn't painfully shifting as if she'd just been torn apart. Reva was lighter and freer than ever before.

With wide eyes, she clasped Crow's warm and delicious hands. "I think we should dance. In the water. On top of the sun. Within the stars. And shine and shine and shine."

"Brighter," he said softly, stroking a thumb against her wrist, leaning closer. He chewed on his bottom lip.

Reva remembered the Gnome King again, but she didn't care about seeing him anymore. Or Locasta. She wanted to stay here beside the river with Crow, where they could run amuck, chase each other, and dance. Except they had too much clothing on. Why had she even gotten dressed?

Reva's gaze fell to the tan skin of Crow's throat. She leaned closer, until the tip of her nose pressed to the flesh of his warm neck, and inhaled his scent. From that single touch, she could feel his breaths. Him breathing into her, her breathing into him. He smelled so good, so fresh, like the forest.

"Reva," he rasped. "Please kiss me. Kiss me so I don't forget you."

Why would he forget her? "Stop being so silly," she said, rubbing her head along his bare shoulder. She could never forget him. But she had before... Green. Green. Green. Everything was green. Everything had hurt. Hurt. Hurt.

No more games.

Grabbing the sides of Crow's face, she straightened on her knees. "Don't let me forget you either."

His lips parted as her mouth crashed into his. And she pulled him toward her, one arm entwined and clutching his hair while the other gripped the bare skin of his back. Crow inhaled sharply before his lips finally moved against hers, like he was trying to remember how to do that too. Their mouths discovered each other as if it were new—she'd never felt so high before. Not even after their drunken night at the Summer Solstice.

Whatever was coursing through her body only heated it more and more. The world turned and turned as she kissed and kissed him, their tongues dancing, their upper bodies swaying. The only thing missing was music. But as Crow lifted her onto his lap and lowered them to the ground, fiddles played in her head.

Every hard inch of him was touching her, and her hand wanted to go straight to the part she hadn't seen, or felt, in so long. She continued to kiss him, allowing her fingers to venture between his legs, then stroking them against his perfect cock through his pants. Reva kissed her way down to the side of his neck, right behind his ear. She moved her hand up his naked chest, feeling each taut muscle connect with her fingertips, when she noticed his body was still, unmoving. Her head jerked up, making everything spin like before, and she found Crow's eyes shut.

"Crow?" she tried to yell, but it came out too tired to be more than a whisper. Her fingers reached under his nose, his warm breath hitting her fingers. He was *sleeping*.

A game of sleeping! She would love a sleeping game much more than the kissing and touching one, especially as her body grew heavier with each passing moment.

Reva pressed herself into Crow, slinging his arm over her so it draped around her waist, before resting her face in the crook of his neck.

They should be continuing somewhere over the rainbow, but she didn't care when she closed her eyes, because sleeping with Crow was her rainbow.

CHAPTER THIRTEEN

CROW

A heavy limb pressed down on Crow's abdomen and a rock jabbed at the center of his back. He yawned and opened his eyes, squinting. The sun was rising, chasing away the night. "Fuck," he shouted, sitting up too quickly. His head spun. "*Fuck*."

A groan came from beside him. "What?"

Reva. Fuzzy memories flooded through Crow. His mind slipping away. Reva bathing. Him crawling like a fool. Reva *kissing* him. Sleep. Them waking to the sound of howling pixies and scrambling to find shelter in the woods like two drunkards. Sleeping again. Her arms around him. Her head on his chest.

"What happened?" Reva asked, groggy.

Crow rolled from beneath the shelter and stood. Sticks were woven together and fastened over four low posts to mimic the appearance of dirt from above. Or, close enough to dirt to fool the pixies. He searched the wooded area around them to avoid meeting Reva's heavy stare. She'd watched him break down, seen his fear. It felt shameful. He wanted Reva to see him as someone she could rely on, not a babbling idiot. It was bad enough the rest of Oz had seen him at his worst, but he wasn't cursed anymore. It was *him* this time. His cheeks burned.

"We left our supplies near the river." She stepped up to his side and ran a hand down her cheek. "Any chance you remember where that river is?"

Crow cringed. "I barely remember us waking up and finding this place." *And the softness of her lips against his.* But he didn't dare say that. Did she remember? Even if she did, she would surely prefer to forget it had happened.

Reva stretched her back and sighed heavily. "This way," she said, sounding mostly certain.

Crow studied the woods as he followed her, hoping to see something familiar. Purple flowers grew up from beneath a carpet of fallen leaves and nearly-invisible hanging vines captured the light, casting prisms over the dark tree bark. The body of a half-eaten fae lay partially under a large bush, too far decomposed to tell what it might have been. A tuft of light brown fur clung to a piece of the carcass, and the bones were scored with teeth marks. Bugs and beasts alike stirred for the day, chirps and snorts piercing through the forest around them, but Crow couldn't tell where they were or from which way they had come. What the hell had happened yesterday? One second, they were fine. The next...

"Here it is," Reva called. She had gotten slightly ahead of him and passed through the trees to the riverbank. Crow stepped over a fallen tree, then swerved to avoid stepping in a spot of stagnant mud. She spun to face him, righteous anger written all over her face. "Someone went through our bags."

Crow sprinted to close the distance between them. Their belongings were scattered over the clearing. Fruit—some nothing but a core, others untouched—and clothing were left in the dirt. But why go through their bags if the thief hadn't wanted to take anything important? Crow flicked his wrists to release his blades, in case the danger lingered, and realized his wrists were bare. He hadn't put his weapons back on after bathing in the river.

"Reva—"

She spun around, gripping a young faun by the scruff of his neck. His hooved feet hung off the ground as he bent his arms and legs in a laughing fit. Small antlers barely poked out of his knotted, sandy blond hair and freckles dusted his high cheekbones.

"Explain yourself," Reva ordered the youth. When his wheezy laugh simply continued, she dropped him next to the pit where she'd cooked their meat. Turning to Crow, she motioned to the faun and asked, "Does this look familiar?"

Crow nodded. The fae looked as dazed as he'd felt the day before, but that only made it more worrisome that his weapons were missing. He stalked up to the child and crossed his arms. "Where are my bracers? My knives?"

The faun merely pointed to the log, still laughing, then rolled over onto his hands and knees. He clawed at the air with one of his hands, growling and hissing like a depraved beast, then fell to his side in a fit again.

Crow kept an eye on him while he crouched beside the log. All their weapons were stashed inside the hollowed end. He quickly pulled them out, fitting his bracers back on and returning his knife to his boot. After yanking his shirt over his head, he shoved everything else back into their bags. They'd already lost a day—there was no more time to waste.

"Nothing seems to be missing unless you count all the food he ate," Reva said as Crow stuffed the last piece of uneaten fruit back in his bag.

"No," Crow agreed, throwing his pack onto his back. He returned to the hysterical faun and crouched down to his level. "We aren't angry," he said calmly. At least, *he* wasn't. He'd committed innocent mischief in his youth too. The plates of pastries his neighbor had cooled on her windowsill were nearly always missing one or two desserts when she'd brought them back inside.

Besides, nothing was gone from their packs and they were the ones who had abandoned their belongings to begin with. There was no way the faun could've known they would return when it was possible the cursed pixies had found them. It made sense that he felt comfortable taking what he wanted. "Can you tell us what happened? Why you're acting like this?"

When the child threw his head back in a cackle, Crow noticed a piece of meat stuck between his front teeth. "Reva?" he asked carefully. "Where did you snare that boar yesterday?"

She made a low, thoughtful sound as if trying to remember. "A bit east of here, I think. Why?"

Crow hung his head. That made sense—the family of boars in that part of Oz fed on the poppies that had spread from the yellow brick road into the forest. The animals were well-known to those who traveled as often as Crow did. If they weren't passed out among the poppies, they were running wild while high, and there was no helping anyone caught picking their precious flowers. Why Reva hadn't hunted closer to the river where the boars ate mostly mushrooms was a moot point now—they'd eaten tainted meat without realizing it.

"Why?" Reva repeated when he didn't answer.

"The boars there eat poppies," he said in a low voice. There had been an unfortunate incident years ago where he'd tripped over one of the boars a few yards away from the poppies. The group had flown into hysterics, some so badly that they'd passed out, while several others must've had a bad reaction. Crow had to fly out of there before they'd trampled him.

Reva plopped onto the log, staring down at her hands. He thought she was going to burst into tears when a bark of laughter escaped her.

"Thank fucking goodness!" she said, jerking her head up to peer at the sky. "Being drunk over a few poppies is better than being cursed again. But I still don't have my magic back."

Crow eased out of his crouch and sank down beside her, watching the child giggle to himself. He had thought his curse was returning too. The poppies had fogged his mind. Everything that should've been important had flown straight out of his brain until all that was left were pure emotions. "I share that sentiment."

Reva shifted next to him and Crow knew she was about to bring up their kiss. "We acted like that for a reason."

"We didn't lose our minds," Crow said in a flat voice. He didn't dare look at her, but he hoped she took the hint. Poppies or not, he didn't feel like celebrating. It *had* felt as if his mind was slipping away. He shook away the flicker of fear. "We should sit with the youngling until he's better."

"That could take all day," she argued. "We don't have that kind of time."

"If our daughter was in this situation, we would want someone to protect her." He turned to face Reva, but his eyes only reached her chin. He'd done what he could for Thelia after she arrived in Oz—guided her as best he could with his broken mind. All of the times he *wasn't* able to shield her still haunted him though. As did the moments he'd missed. "We're staying."

CHAPTER FOURTEEN

REVA

Reva stared at the sleeping faun in her lap. His clothing was full of tears and splattered with dried dirt. There were light scratches on his cheeks and he looked like he hadn't seen a home in weeks. She and Crow had been watching over him for what felt like seasons upon seasons, when in fact it had only been perhaps half a day.

The child had passed out from delirium. Crow had caught him after the faun had leapt from the forest floor and tried to scale a tree while laughing. His eyes had shut mid-climb and he'd fallen backward, right into Crow's waiting arms. But Reva didn't want the child to have to sleep on the hard earth, so she let his head rest in her lap while his knees hugged his chest. She wondered what it would have been like to hold Thelia when her daughter was this age. He appeared the same age that Thelia had been when she'd first come to Oz, so perhaps somewhere between eleven and twelve years old.

Reva hummed a song for him as she brushed her fingers through his tangled locks of blond hair. Poppies were dangerous, but especially for anyone who wasn't fully grown. She was surprised the poppies hadn't ended his life, but he must not have eaten much of the boar.

Smoke wafted around her, and the roasting scent of meat hit her nose. Reva's stomach rumbled with hunger as she peered over her shoulder and watched Crow char an owl over a fire he'd built.

"Are you sure this one isn't filled with poppies too?" Reva asked, not really caring, because it smelled divine.

"I'm sure." Crow winked. "Birds are smart. They know not to eat poppies."

"Hmm. You're part bird and yet you still didn't detect it in the meat before." Her eyes darted to Crow's mouth, lingering before flicking away. She told herself they had just drifted there because she was thinking about him eating the meat. Not him kissing her. Or Gods, her kissing him first… Even though she'd been drunk out of her wits on poppies, she still remembered the softness of his mouth on hers. Her hands in his hair, his hands on her lower back. How hard he'd been.

Reva yearned for him the way she always had, and this was why she hadn't wanted him to come with her on this journey. Because he could indeed always win her over in the end. No matter how hard she tried not to be won.

A soft mewl came from the faun. Perhaps he would be stirring soon. She hoped.

"Here," Crow said, lifting a piece of blackened meat and lightly blowing on it. He started to give it to her and noticed her hands were still occupied with the child. "Part your lips."

She was too hungry to say no. As she opened her mouth, he placed the tender meat on her tongue, his fingers brushing her lips as he released it. There wasn't a grassy flavor like the day before, which she now chalked up to the poppies. It was savory and practically fell apart as she chewed.

"So," he said, taking a seat beside her and plopping a slice of meat into his mouth.

"So," she repeated, choosing to stare at the river instead of at Crow.

Before they could play their echo game anymore, another sound came from the child. His lids slowly opened to reveal orange irises and large pupils. When his gaze met theirs, his eyes widened. With a loud screech, he jerked up flailing, spitting, and flapping his arms to find balance. Was he still out of his mind? He pulled out a tiny blade from the back of his pants and held it up. Reva wanted to roll her eyes because she could easily kick it out of his hand before the youngling could even make another move. But she decided to let the faun have his moment, and Crow seemed to think the same, as he just crossed his arms and studied him.

A distressed expression crossed the child's face, his pale coloring becoming green. Dropping the knife, he turned around and expelled whatever had been in his stomach.

The faun stumbled backward and almost fell. Crow caught him like he had earlier that day. "We're not going to hurt you."

Reva scooped up the child's weapon, knelt in front of him, and held his blade up—with the handle toward him—to grab. "He's right. We're trying to help you. Now, where are your parents?"

The faun's bottom lip trembled as his hand shakily took the knife. "They're dead."

Reva slowly nodded in understanding. Since she'd been away, many children were without their parents or vice versa. Too many dead and too many separated. But when she was the Wicked Witch of the West, she'd separated families, too. She tried not to think of the blood she'd shed as she asked, "What's your name?"

His fingers gripped his blade, knuckles white. "Birch."

"I'm sorry, Birch." She knew she shouldn't say her name just yet, but she wanted to give him something. He was too young to remember her from before anyway. "I'm Reva and this is Crow."

Birch's gaze snapped to Crow's, recognizing his name, but

hers must have indeed been forgotten with time, since no one had been allowed to use it in years. "Locasta killed my parents. She said she would protect us and she didn't. She's turning on anyone who speaks up. My parents wanted her to end the assault on the Emerald City, and she refused."

Reva pressed her lips together and shook her head. "She is never to be trusted."

So the Northern bitch wasn't pretending to be good anymore. It seemed she thought her victory was near. If Reva's magic didn't return soon, Locasta may very well be victorious and rule over the Land of Oz. But no—Thelia was stronger than Locasta. Reva had felt Thelia's magic when it drew Reva and Ozma out from the dark place, had seen the strength in it. Yet it would take a while for Thelia to learn how to wield it at will.

The child was now studying Crow in awe, his hand no longer shaking. Perhaps she did need Crow after all. Everyone in Oz still looked up to him, to Thelia. Reva related most to the Tin WoodsMan in this quest, only her nature was even more questionable. Tin could be forgiven, but would the fae of Oz ever forgive her for what she'd done?

Birch needed to go somewhere safe, but there wasn't a trustworthy town nearby to take him to. The Emerald City had the tavern, but Birch actually making it there without someone killing him might be too tricky. Reva and Crow couldn't drag him through the cornfield on their way to the Gnome King either. He would be tortured.

An idea came to her then. One that would be perfect, and possibly selfish. But Birch was from the North and if he could learn to trust the other territories then maybe other Northerners would too... "How would you feel about going to the South?"

All the color drained from Birch's face. He rubbed the back of his neck and bit at his bottom lip. "Langwidere is there."

"She's dead," said Crow. "It's safe now."

"What if we told you it was now a haven?" Reva started. "That you could go to the palace and be safe. Crow and I will be helping to make the North safe as well."

"Glinda would never help the North."

"No. Not Glinda, but someone who loves all of Oz. She now rules the South and the West, and was a child like you when she saved us once before."

Birch lifted his chin, his blond brows all the way up his forehead. "Who is this you speak of?"

"Have you heard of a human girl named Dorothy?"

She'd expected him to look pleased, not narrow his eyes with distrust. "She's the cause of all this. The reason everyone's dead. That's what Locasta said."

And Locasta had murdered his parents, but she couldn't word it like that. "Do you believe everything Locasta says? Dorothy killed Langwidere and is now going to help rebuild the South. *We* trust her. Am I so bad? Is Crow so bad?"

Birch scanned her up and down. "I don't know." This was taking up too much time, and she needed him to head South already.

"Couldn't I have hurt you in your sleep if I truly wanted you dead?" she asked. "Couldn't I have left you here all alone and not given you this opportunity?"

"I suppose." Birch pursed his lips in a thin line. "Dorothy really is good, then?"

"The purest of hearts." A much better one than she, Reva, could ever have. "Are you brave enough to head to the South, her palace, alone?"

Straightening his shoulders, and lengthening his spine, he puffed up his chest. "I've been on my own for a while now and have been surviving just fine. Until I ate that meat..."

Gently, Reva placed a hand on his shoulder. "Avoid going through the Emerald City."

Crow pulled an apple from his bag and handed it to Birch. "For the road." Reva wanted to rip the fruit from his hand and give him a different one, but the child needed it more than her.

Reva removed her palm from his shoulder. "Dorothy will

need a good guard, and I think you're just the fae to help her rebuild from the destruction Langwidere has caused."

"I'll do it."

She knew Dorothy would welcome him as soon as he showed up on her doorstep.

"And, Birch, if you help our daughter succeed, then we'll be most grateful," Reva added.

"Daughter?" His face was full of surprise. "Dorothy's your daughter? But you're..." Birch looked at Crow. "He's... She's..."

"She's not human. Not really. She's fae, like us."

Birch studied his small hands, his brow furrowed as he peered back up at them. "I'll protect the daughter of Crow with my life. My parents told me to never make promises unless I mean them, and I mean it."

"You will be rewarded." She would make sure of it.

Crow pointed him in the direction of the yellow brick road and told him to remain on it as he headed south, except for the capital, which he needed to go around.

Birch turned away from them and took off in the southern direction without a glance back, not appearing the least bit afraid. Perhaps he'd already lost too much to be fearful.

"You didn't mention that Tin would be there," Crow said, stepping up beside Reva.

"I didn't want to frighten him. Thelia will help him understand. Besides, Tin wasn't as awful as me. He didn't kill for pure pleasure."

"It wasn't *you* doing it, though."

"I know," she whispered. "But it still hurts. It always will."

"Reva?"

She peered up at him. "Yes?"

"I promise not to leave you behind again. And if I could have come with you to the dark place, I would have. Even if it had to be for all eternity." Something nudged her fingertips. Crow had pushed an apple into her palm. "I didn't give Birch the last one."

Her heart thundered in her chest at his words. She lifted the fruit to her lips, and couldn't help but smile as she bit into the sweet juiciness.

Without another word, they adjusted their packs and drank from the river before continuing their journey. There wasn't much daylight left, but they could hopefully make it to the outskirts of the cornfield before dusk.

After pushing several branches aside, Reva and Crow entered an area with trees of white. But it wasn't the bark that made them that color—the entirety of the trunks and limbs were wrapped in ivory spider silk. A scream sounded above them, and Reva peered up to find a large spider with long, thin legs rolling a sprite into its web. *Good.* That species of sprite was a nuisance, using their fangs to suck blood from young fae and take bites from their flesh.

As more and more spiders poked out from places draped among the trees, Reva's instinct was to use her magic. But it still wouldn't spark to life. The spiders didn't venture any closer. Something told her that they recognized her as Reva, the ruler of the West, not as the Wicked Witch, and they knew better than to make a move.

Reva and Crow traveled in comfortable silence. She still couldn't help but think about yesterday, with the kiss—she needed to stop and not dwell on it. At least not until after what they needed to do was done.

She brushed away branches of tall leafy bushes, and up ahead, a silhouette spread like floating shadows swaying back and forth. The setting sun's rays shifted as they approached, revealing the cornfield. The field went on and on. It would take them forever to cross through it, so they would need to find somewhere within the field itself to stay the night the following evening. For now, they could find somewhere at its edge.

But as she shielded her eyes from the sun, she noticed something new. The once-yellow and green stalks, though still tall, had turned entirely black. The smell of rot permeated the air, making her almost lose her stomach's contents. As Reva and Crow stepped closer, she noticed yellowed skeletons, covered in dust, sprawled about the ground at strange angles.

"Was it like this when you were here?" Reva's voice came out angry, but not at Crow. At whoever had done this.

She whirled to face him when his answer remained tucked away. Something in his face appeared stricken, broken.

"Crow?"

He shook his head. "It was bad when I was here, but nothing like this."

CHAPTER FIFTEEN

CROW

Crow lay on his back, staring up at the cloudless sky. Millions of stars glimmered down upon the small camp he and Reva had set up. There was no fire for warmth, or to reduce the risk of night beasts finding them, but anxiety left him feeling uncomfortably warm, his muscles quivering at the nearness of the cornfield. It was right there—on the other side of the trees... He hadn't even been able to swallow the fruit Reva had sliced for him. She'd done it just the way he liked, too—thin but still thick enough to get a small crunch.

"You should sleep," Reva said softly.

His wife sat on a large boulder, facing out toward the cornfield, and cleaned her nails with the tip of Crow's knife. She looked so beautiful in the moonlight that it hurt, but his gaze kept trying to search for danger beyond her. In the field. In *his* field. A shudder ran through his body and he focused on his hands.

"I'll keep watch for enemies," she added.

He shook his head. "You should rest. I won't be able to sleep anyway."

"Try," she ordered.

Crow gave her the smallest of smiles. "I would usually make an inuendo here, but I'm afraid I'm all out of them at the moment."

Reva rolled her eyes and tucked his knife into her boot. "Why don't you tell me a story instead?"

"What kind of story?"

"About what happened to your wings," she said without looking at him.

Ah. That. He hesitated. She wouldn't like it—Locasta's name seemed enough to set off her anger—but if she wanted to know… "After exhausting every lead in an attempt to locate the human Dorothy, I went to see Locasta. She'd had Whispa exchange Thelia with the mortal baby, so I figured she would have some idea where to look—maybe the real Dorothy had been enchanted as a palace slave or given to another family. I don't know. It was foolish. When she finally realized I was only there for news of the girl and not to reconcile, she forced me to transform and snapped my wings. Then she tossed me down the stairs, where I barely managed to remain conscious long enough to shift back. Then one of her human changelings helped me escape, but he didn't make it…" He would spare Reva the little details, like the sound of his bird bones breaking, the intense pain that made white flash before his eyes, or the human's agonizing screams.

Reva sat thoughtfully for a moment before saying, "Sleep, Crow."

He shifted to his side to better see his wife. Just as he was about to insist that he take the first watch, she began to hum quietly so only he could hear. It was the slow melody of a Western song, full of drawn-out notes. Her voice was gentle and soft as it wove a wordless tale. Crow instantly relaxed as Reva's voice flowed over him. Closing his eyes, he let the music wrap around him like a blanket. He could have almost cried with relief

116

in that split second before sleep took him. Because if he was sleeping, he wasn't thinking about the path through the corn that they had to take the next morning.

Crow stood at the edge of the cornfield, along with Reva, at the first light of dawn. He fought the urge to run from the place Locasta had trapped him all those years ago—to fly away from this horrible, cursed place. Spreading his broken wings and forcing them to carry him into the air would've been less painful than taking another step forward.

The stalks making up his former prison bars were no longer golden. They didn't sway in the breeze as they used to or carry the earthy scent which somehow still clung to him. The rustling of leaves that used to be his constant companion—a song seemingly sung just for him as he suffered through his days on the post—no longer filled the air.

Now, the field was as black as death and smelled of decomposing bodies. The ground, once rich, brown soil, had become dry and cracked. White worms crept over the fallen, rotting husks, and, beneath the outer layers, so many wriggled that it looked as if the corn were alive.

"You'll have to lead the way," Reva said, straightening her shoulders.

Crow jumped at the sound of her voice. "What?"

"You know the field, right? I don't want to get us lost and spend more time in there than we need to."

"Right." *Right.* It was a giant cornfield with no actual pathways. The trails that did exist were created by fae stomping through the field to find their way blindly to the other side, resulting in a maze of twists and turns. Going around it would take far too long. And yet... He spun to face Reva and reached out to her, freezing before he could grab her arms. "The thing is, when I was in there before, I wasn't in my right mind. And...

And I wasn't, you know…" He'd spent eleven years tied to a wooden post until Thelia had happened upon him. She'd braved the field just to help him when she'd heard him crying in the distance. His legs trembled, remembering how weak they'd been when she'd cut him down as Toto barked at her side. "I wasn't mobile."

Reva studied his face. "We have to go through," she said, her expression soft.

"I know." Crow squeezed his eyes shut and steeled his nerves. He could do this. It would be fine. "Let's be quick about it then."

"As fast as our feet can carry us," she promised.

Crow adjusted his mask and extended his blades over his hands—it was better to be prepared for the worst. After bouncing on the balls of his feet for a handful of moments, he let out a harsh breath and barreled into the rotting cornfield. If he'd tried to walk at a leisurely pace, he never would've made it. Especially not when the stalks left a foul-smelling residue wherever they brushed against him. His stomach rolled when he noticed liquid oozing down each of the husks.

"Th-there's a shed at the center of the field," he said in a shaky voice. He'd told Reva as much the night before, but talking seemed to help his nerves. "If we can make it there today, that's halfway to the other side."

"We'll make it there before dark," Reva reassured him.

The patience in her voice continued to surprise him. He kept expecting her to snap at him to get over his fear or to stop talking, but this side of Reva was the one he knew best—the one she had only showed him behind closed doors. The fae of the West loved and respected her, but she'd still always felt the need to show them she was a strong leader. Strong leaders were kind without being soft, or so Reva had repeatedly claimed. He liked her softness though.

The sun beamed down on them as they walked farther and farther, seeming like they would never make it to the halfway point. They only stopped to relieve themselves. Crow's heart wouldn't stop racing, though it wasn't solely due to his past. Petrified corpses were entwined in the stalks. Elves and gnomes, goblins and kobolds, all with their mouths frozen open in horror. Their skin had blackened and become leathery, their milky-white eyes wide. The only thing that gave Crow any hint about how long the dead had been there was the state of their clothing. While some hung in tatters, others were relatively clean and intact, which begged the question—how had they become mummified so quickly?

"I don't like this," Reva whispered at his side. "You said it wasn't like this before, right? Do you know what lives here now?"

Crow squinted as he tried to remember. After spending so long trying to forget, it wasn't easy to recall specifics of the days he'd been trapped here. But there was no imminent danger that came to him—at least none that frequented the field. He recalled seeing a giant and a redcap once or twice, though they'd barely spared him a glance despite his cries for help. Dorothy had been the exception.

"I've never seen it like this," Crow finally said. The corn had never withered, and no one had ever come to tend the crop. It was always simply there. A cursed place, always with a cursed soul to watch over it. Locasta had killed his predecessor, but there was no way of knowing the current resident. And he hadn't dared to look at the post rising from the field's center to see who kept the vigil now. "Something must've happened after I left."

Reva held her hands up, trying in vain to get them to spark. "I have a bad feeling about this."

She wasn't alone—Crow felt as if the corn itself were watching them. The sensation of eyes bored into his back, but it was nothing compared to the painful twisting of his stomach. Reva walked close enough to offer her support without making him feel like there wasn't room to defend himself if they were ambushed. To defend them both.

"The shed isn't far now," he said after what felt like a lifetime.

Crow swallowed hard. The shed was close, but his old post was even closer. He never wanted to lay eyes on it again. His heart battered the inside of his chest, harder and harder. He wasn't normally afraid of anything, but this … this… *No,* his mind screamed. Their shelter was only a dozen or so rows away. Beyond the…

The…

"Crow?" Reva put a hand on one of his bracers. The blades were extended, though he couldn't remember doing that. "Are you all right?"

Fuck. He was as far from all right as a fae could get. His throat was so tight that words refused to pass, and his mouth felt so dry he thought his tongue would crack. He stumbled away from Reva and through the final row between him and a twenty-foot post—a disturbingly *empty* post. Where was the scarecrow? There was *always* a scarecrow. How did his replacement escape his or her magic tethering? The post's wood was aged and full of tiny holes from insects. When it held him, the post had been pristine. At the top, a horizontal beam formed a T. Iron circles—now rusted—stuck from the posts where rope had once been attached, holding Crow in place for over a decade. His mind reeled and swirled until his thoughts became jumbled. If he wasn't careful, this *place* would ruin him in a way no curse ever could.

Reva stepped lightly up to his side. "Don't look at it…"

Crow felt the blood drain from his face. The post seemed to call to him like an old friend, but that was a lie. It was his enemy. A beast waiting to gobble him up. Still, his feet moved to its base. A shaky breath fell from between his lips as his hand rose to caress the wood.

The moment his fingertips made contact, his body went rigid. His mind was completely blank. A buzzing emptiness swept through him as the world spun. Or was he spinning? His back was suddenly on the ground. A dull ache throbbed in his head. Was it from the fall? Or the … the…

No words came to Crow then. Only pictures. Images of his past. A beautiful female. A baby. Another beautiful female with a cruel smile. Feathers. Feathers falling. Bones breaking. *He* was breaking.

"Crow!"

His eyes snapped open to find a female haloed by the setting sun. He blinked. Blinked again. Her face was white with worry, pupils blown wide, breath coming fast. Another blink. *Reva.* He recognized her. Loved her.

"Can you hear me?" She tugged him into a sitting position. "Are you all right? Say something."

"Reva," he breathed.

"Yes," she said with a weak smile. "That's right. I'm Reva. And you're Crow."

Crow. That was his name. She was right.

A black bird cawed overhead, and Crow followed its movement with a bitter feeling in his gut. *Fly.* He wanted to fly. The bird swooped down before them and exploded into a puff of black smoke. When it cleared, a gorgeous female in a green dress stood before them. Had he ever beheld such magnificence? She was flawless, with dark, shimmering hair, ruby red lips, and a smooth complexion. Crow's blood warmed as she took a few sultry steps forward, her cloven hooves leaving small grooves in the hard dirt.

"Crow?" she asked in the sweetest of voices. "I assume you to be *the* Crow who was trapped here?"

Trapped. Crow's lungs constricted as he tried to pull in another breath. His mind struggled against an invisible binding, locking his reasoning away.

"It seems this field traded one bird for another." The female's eyes flicked to Reva. "I'm the Baobhan sith. And you—"

"Fuck off," Reva clipped.

"Oh, dear." The Baobhan sith circled them predatorily. "You are both trespassing."

Crow shivered. His cock grew hard as the Baobhan sith ran a hand slowly down her body, caressing each curve. But wanting her was dangerous, wasn't it? This female meant them harm. So, why didn't he want to fight her? To protect Reva and himself? He only wanted himself inside the luscious female. Wanted her naked body straddling his, covered in sweat, stroking, touching, touching...

"As I'm sure you saw, I do not allow such offenses to go unpunished." The Baobhan sith smirked knowingly at Crow. Pointed canines poked over her bottom lip. "But I will deal with *you* later so we have time to enjoy ourselves first."

"Like hell you will!" Reva snarled.

The Baobhan sith lunged, her mouth open, fangs glinting. Crow looked down at his hands. Blades should've been there. A hiss filled his ears—the Baobhan sith, he guessed. Because Reva didn't *hiss*. He shook his hands, hoping the blades would appear. How did they work?

"Reva?" he called. "Do you know how to—"

The field exploded with green light. The magic tingled against Crow's skin and burned through a layer of the fog engulfing his brain. He gasped as information slipped through the cracks. He was Crow. She was Reva. Dorothy was Thelia. They were going to kill Locasta. Because they had a plan. Of some sort. Crow scrambled to his feet, desperately searching for a weak spot in the fog clouding his mind, where he could pull out something else. Anything else.

His gaze drifted up and caught on smoke curling toward the sky from the twitching body of the fanged female. Dead. *Maybe dead.* The limbs still moved. Dead meant still. He cocked his head thoughtfully. *Almost dead*, he decided after a moment. That seemed right. He puffed his chest, proud of himself for coming to a conclusion, and looked over the body to Reva. The sight of her made his cock throb. *That's right.* He didn't want to fuck the

Baobhan sith at all—because he already loved *this* female.

"What's going on with you?" Reva asked, breathless from the brief battle.

"I…"

Reva studied him for a long moment. "We need to get to that shed."

"There." Crow pointed to the top of the roof, barely visible over the blackened stalks. He knew that answer—that was good. He knew things! But why did it feel so bad to be so pleased with himself? His head throbbed painfully, and another thought snuck through. *You're cursed.* His stomach twisted. *No.* This wasn't his curse. Because his curse wouldn't allow him to reason out problems. It wouldn't allow him to think at all. Or remember. And he remembered Reva. His wife. *My wife!* He was a lucky male. But he hadn't seen her in a long time. She didn't like him much anymore. He scowled at the vague memory of her walking away from him at Glinda's palace.

Reva stepped toward him as if she were going to comfort him, but he shuffled back before she could. He didn't want to be consoled when his mind was so scrambled, especially not by her. "Shed," he said, and marched toward it.

Chapter Sixteen

Reva

Reva watched as Crow awkwardly marched to the shed, his arms swaying differently than usual. Even his pace was off. If she didn't know better, she would have thought he was delirious from poppies again. But this was something else.

"Crow!" she shouted. "Stop!" His body came to an abrupt halt. He remained still, as though he were ready to obey her next command. Crow's head tilted toward the clouds in wonder, his jaw hanging open. Something in this field was causing him to not be himself. Locasta must not have only put a curse on him—but connected him to the field as well. Even though he'd been gone, replaced by a new guard, he still seemed to be linked to it somehow.

The trickle of thunder pulsed through Reva's veins, her magic stirring. It had come back, just in time to kill that bitch. She knew all about Baobhan siths. They would seduce a victim, making them feel good, aroused, loved, then rip their throat apart, draining all their blood. When she'd seen Crow's cock unwillingly harden in his pants because of the female, she'd known there was only one thing to do. Kill her. Even if she had to do it with her hands. Perhaps it was pure emotion that made her magic come forward—*finally*—when she'd needed it.

Crow was still staring up at the clouds. Had he done this most of the time when he was here, attached to that pole? She grabbed him by the elbow and tugged him toward the darkened shed straight ahead. "Try not to talk … or get distracted by the clouds."

"Um." He released a chuckle but let her continue to lead him.

As she pushed a few blackened stalks out of the way, reeking of filth, the shed came into full view.

She sucked in a sharp breath and Crow covered his mouth. "It's dead. It's dead."

What he meant was that the entirety of the shed was covered in blackened skin and she could *smell* it. But it wasn't a whole sheet of skin wrapped around the building. Strips from what she assumed were numerous fae's flesh had been stitched together across the outside walls of the shed. Disgust filled her. Once Reva killed Locasta, the curse on the cornfield could possibly be lifted. What else had this bitch destroyed in Oz?

Around the field, birds cawed, their sounds echoing in all directions around them. She wondered if they were Locasta's minions or just kept to themselves. Either way, she and Crow would need to stay silent.

A strong breeze blew across the cornfield, shaking the stalks and rumpling her hair. The Baobhan sith was dead. Would another one be coming?

Straightening her shoulders, Reva grabbed the handle of the door. The texture beneath her fingertips squished when she turned the knob. The door creaked slightly as she pushed it open. She expected the inside to reek of dead flesh too, but it didn't. The scent of sweet pastries clouded the air and light shone through the two rectangular windows, cascading its glow over the area.

In the center of the room was a table and four chairs with a full meal spread across the top. She turned to Crow who was hungrily staring at the food.

"Is it edible?" she asked while sweeping her gaze over the area. A bed with a cream crocheted blanket was in the corner and not much else.

"Dorothy ate here," he finally said, and took a seat at the table in front of buttered rolls, juicy meats, jellied pastries, and glasses of wine.

He was back to calling their daughter *Dorothy*. Reva sighed as he started to stuff his mouth with pastries. Smacking and smacking, his sounds made her shake her head.

Ten years ago, when Crow had been with Thelia, he'd never once shifted, because his mind hadn't allowed him to remember. Not until the Wizard broke his curse. Thelia had told her that much. Perhaps if his magic was back the way hers was, he could shift and that could possibly snap him out of it.

Sinking down in the chair beside Crow, Reva leaned forward and pressed her hands against his warm cheeks, feeling the curves of his high cheekbones, then turned his head to face her. He stopped chewing as she studied the scar across his nose, his lips reddened from the jam, and the glaze in his stare that wasn't fully Crow.

"Can you try and shift now?" she asked slowly to make sure he could understand her. "My magic has returned and that has to mean yours has as well."

He tilted his head, eyes seeming to dance as he studied her.

The Wizard had fixed him the last time. What if Crow could never shift again? What if he was like this permanently? *No.* She reminded herself that this was linked to Locasta. He wouldn't always be this way. Perhaps she should have him remain in this shelter while she went to the Gnome King and Locasta. No to that too. She remembered how angry she'd been when Crow had left her at the tavern. Seeing him so unlike himself, defenseless, made her realize that she couldn't abandon him, especially not here.

"You're a bird. Think about your arms becoming wings, your body covered in feathers, having a beak, and being the color of the night sky. Imagine yourself whole, flying through the wind, above the clouds." Reva would lie in the field near her palace, watching him circle around her, bringing small gifts— meaningless to others, but everything to her. Berries, twigs in the shape of rings, hair pieces created from leaves.

He pursed his lips. "A bird. Dorothy liked birds."

She had to do it, had to use his true name this one time. Besides, he'd used hers, so it was only fair. "Crowestyn Sennan Noloris, I command you to shift into your bird form."

His brown eyes shut as soon as she finished using his beautiful name. A flash of darkened smoke came, stronger than it ever had before. He was no longer directly in front of her, but below her. Dark and perfect, his feathered wings tucked against his fragile body, no longer dragging.

"Crowestyn Sennan Noloris, I release you." She prayed to the gods above that he would understand her. "Do you remember everything?" she asked hesitantly, kneeling to where there was barely any space between her face and his.

Crow looked up at her, his small, beady eyes meeting hers, then nodded.

Lifting one of his feathery wings, she stroked the softness, the wholeness. "You aren't broken anymore," she murmured. "The potions worked." Relief washed over her. This was one thing the Wizard had done right—abandoned his potions.

His gaze peered up at the half-eaten jelly pastry.

"Before you try shifting back, finish eating." Reva scooped him up from the floor and set him on the table. He'd had trouble eating in his bird form before, but he was healed now. "I don't want to see any more of your sloppy eating if you aren't yourself again."

Crow's tiny body vibrated, and a high-pitched sound escaped his beak, his way of chuckling. He gave her a wink before he started pecking at the buttery bread. She rolled her eyes and lifted a slice of meat to her mouth. The flavor was a tad bitter, and if she had to guess, she would bet that all the food here was glamoured. At that moment, she didn't care if she was eating leaves, or mud, because it was filling her stomach.

After Crow took a final peck at his meat, he flapped his wings and flew down to the floor.

"Now that your belly is full, try shifting," Reva said, standing and placing her hands on her hips. She hoped to the fae gods that his mind wouldn't revert to her having to watch over him like a child.

A darkened cloud came with a light swish, a few dark feathers falling to the floor. Crow was in front of her, closer than she'd expected. Possibly closer than he'd expected too, because he was silent, not blinking. Staring. Breathing. Saying nothing.

Damnit.

The curse Locasta put on the cornfield must be too strong, and now he was cursed once again. Her heart beat wildly, and she bit her lip so she wouldn't scream. Reva grabbed his cheeks between her palms and pressed her lips to his soft mouth. "Come back to me."

"I just needed to collect myself," Crow murmured against her lips. "That was all."

"You scared me!" Reva snapped, taking a step back. But more than anything, relief washed over her.

"I'd say the kiss was worth it." He smiled and winked.

She couldn't even be mad at him as she glanced out the window. "When we go back into the field, I'm going to have you shift so if anything happens again, at least I can easily carry you instead of dragging you through the corn."

A sizzling sound stirred from outside. She hurried to the window and froze. Dark gray smoke wafted from the ground, making it hard to see. But then something shifted, and she looked in horror as the darkened cornstalks started *moving*, as though they were hands reaching toward the shed to rip off the roof. "What the fuck is happening?" She turned with wide eyes to look back at Crow.

The cornstalks were bending, curving, and creating a barrier around them.

"The corn won't allow us to leave," Crow said, sidling up beside her. "Not until another fae is on the post. It won't take long. I came across that part of the curse while researching and, when one dies or leaves the field, another appears before the next sunrise."

"I'm getting tired of this shit!" Reva stomped toward the table and plopped down onto a chair. "Every second we're delayed is another second Locasta is breathing."

"No one said it would be easy." He rubbed his temple, headed toward the bed, and took a seat. "It's only until morning."

Morning her ass. With narrowed eyes, she watched as he tugged off his boots and fished out a book from his bag.

She took a knife from the table and went to the door, throwing it open. Before her was a barrier of corn—not even a hole she could peep through. The scent of decay struck her and she held her breath. Drawing up her magic, Reva sparked a jolt of lightning toward it. Nothing happened besides the bolt turning to smoke. With the sharp knife clenched in her hand, she tried to slice at the stalks. Nothing. Not even a dent. She released a frustrated noise.

"Are you done trying?" Crow called. "I lived here for eleven years, remember? Fae would pass through on occasion. It may be darker here now, but I still know how the corn works."

Reva crossed the shed and stopped directly in front of him, her shadow covering half his face and book. "How can you just sit here and read?"

He quirked a brow. "It's called a distraction."

She set down the knife on the floor, removed her boots, and took a seat beside him. "But your mind was just affected. Shouldn't you rest?"

"All the more reason to read."

He was worried. That was why he was reading. Perhaps he did need the distraction, but he truly didn't want to lose his mind again. She could relate. As the Wicked Witch, she could think clearly, but she had still, in a way, lost her mind, too.

Taking a deep swallow, she said softly, "Tell me what the story is about."

His eyes shifted to Reva's, and he batted his lashes at her. "A female is annoyed with a male but then she realizes she isn't and they…" Crow trailed off.

He knew she wouldn't leave it at that. "They what?"

"They make love. A lot."

"You're such a liar. Give me that." She yanked the book from his hand and fumbled to straighten it. She read the first page about a large cock and an innocent female orgasming, then tossed it back into his lap because it was indeed one of *those* stories. Reva hated them—she would rather feel the real thing than imagine it.

Crow let out a chuckle, almost musical, filling up the room. "Apologize for calling me a liar."

"I will not." Reva paused, turning serious as she remembered their night in the tavern. "You really didn't lay with another female while I was away?"

"Why would I? You were my wife before and you will always be, even in death." He lifted the book back up.

Reva could feel the heat rolling off her in waves. She took the book from his hand and tossed it to the floor with a heavy thump. "You can't say things like that and just go back to *reading*."

He lifted a brow, waiting for her to continue.

She stared at the planes of his face, the angles, his full lips, his square jaw. Her body heated even more in that moment, a different kind of warmth, flames feeling as though they were licking at her insides. Aware, she was so very aware of every inch of him and his strong, muscular form. Leaning over him, she pressed a hand to his cheek. "Do you think we would still know

130

what to do if we…"

"I would always know what to do with you." With quick reflexes, Crow rolled Reva to her back until he was on top of her, propping himself up on his elbows.

"Hmm, you may have to prove it." In open invitation, Reva spread her legs so that he could settle himself between them. He drew in a sharp breath and so did she when his cock hardened right against the spot that needed him the most. Yet the damn clothing was still in the way.

Reva knew she could hesitate, make him hurt in that moment, say something awful. But she didn't want to. She wasn't angry anymore. Not to say that she wouldn't ever be angry with him again because that would indeed happen, but they'd always been meant for one another. He was the sun and she was the moon and his rays would light the darkness around her. Always. They had both endured enough. And maybe Crow had been through more than her because she'd known he had been alive, while he'd thought she was dead. He'd suffered in the light while she'd suffered in the dark. They were both changed now, but that didn't mean their hearts didn't still beat for one another.

"I love you," she whispered. "Even when I thought I hated you, I loved you. But you never deserved that. You never deserved any of this. And I'm sorry. I'm sorry for—"

His lips fiercely silenced her with a kiss. Her eyes widened in surprise while his shut. She closed hers then, and relaxed into him, his touch, his movements. She tasted him as he deepened the kiss, and she devoured it, his familiar flavor along with the jellied desserts. Crow's tongue entangled with hers and he nipped softly at her lower lip. She forgot how Crow's kisses felt—as good as if she'd just been fucked. She'd kissed him after the poppies, and the soft kiss when she thought he'd still been cursed, but this was different. This was a true kiss.

Reva drew him closer, her hands venturing up the smoothness of his back to the ripples across his chest. There were too many layers of clothing between them and she wanted them all off.

As she reached for his pants, he yanked at her shirt and corset. Their breaths came out heavy, desperate. Everything was shed, their lips never once leaving one another's, as if those body parts had known the painful abandonment of years separated from each other as keenly as their owners.

Their naked bodies pressed against one another and she couldn't control a shiver at how good it felt. As she kissed down his salty neck, Reva glided her fingertips to between his legs and gripped his hardened length. She stroked and she stroked. It was so familiar, like they'd never been apart.

Crow groaned and lifted his head, giving her more access to the place behind his ear where she licked and nipped.

His cock throbbed in her hand and she shifted him to his back so she was straddling him. He quickly sat up and adjusted her so she was flush against his chest, her nipples pebbling more than they already had.

"You're beautiful," she whispered as she trailed a finger down the light scar of his nose.

"That was supposed to be my line." He winked, placing his mouth around her nipple, licking, while he cradled the other.

The caresses, touches, and her hips rocking kept coming until she needed more, had to have *much* more.

Crow's hand drifted down between her legs, rubbing in blissful circles, her wetness pooling around his fingertips. "I'm going to please you more than I ever have," he rasped.

Reva arched her back and moaned as he pressed on her center. "Get inside me already," she said, unable to control the need in her voice. "We've waited long enough." Then she lowered herself to her back, taking him with her, his lips tasting hers once more.

"I love you," he murmured. With a single thrust, the way she liked, he pushed into her, filling her, making her gasp. As a lover, Crow always knew how to make her want more of him, even when she'd never planned to fall for him the way she had in their past.

He started pumping his hips, lighting up the nerve endings inside her entire body, creating a starry sky within her darkness. Reva grabbed his ass, driving him to move harder and harder, shaking the entire bed.

When that position fulfilled its duty, Crow lifted her with a firm swoop so that she was straddling him again. The friction increased and she kept her pace as they both sat up, his strong arms holding her tight, while he and his cock ravished her.

Reva's hands cupped his face. Their sweat-slick chests pressed together. The intense sensation was unfurling, like a flower opening and opening, until Reva gasped. The pleasure took over her entire body, vibrating it like thunder, more so than her own magic ever had.

Crow's hands tightened on her hips as she rode him even harder, knowing his satisfaction was nearing by the way he licked his lower lip. "Reva," he rasped when his orgasm followed suit.

Neither one moved from their position, their breaths coming out heavy. They stared at each other, and before tears could form, she put her lips to his, holding them there, thinking, for the first time, about not their past, but their future.

"We'll get back everything we had," Reva swore as her lips left Crow's. "And it will be better than before because we have Thelia with us again."

"We will." He lowered them to the mattress, and she placed her head on his chest, right on the spot where she could hear the musical sound of his heartbeat.

It was too early to sleep and she wanted more of him, not only the physical, but from his lovely mind, his voice. "Tell me about everything you did while I was away." She wanted to hear his entire story, the way she'd heard Thelia's. Not just the bits and pieces that she'd learned about. "Then, afterward, I'm going to make you forget you were ever cursed."

CHAPTER SEVENTEEN

CROW

A loud thud woke Crow with a start. He sat up to find Reva dressed from the waist down as she searched the shed. Crow leaned back on his elbows, completely unbothered by his own nudity, and watched as she kicked a chair aside, grumbling. She had been just as feisty the night before too, her lips around his cock while she gripped his ass. Crow grinned at the memory of having her again. She had tasted like he'd remembered—sweet, yet tart—and had felt even better.

As if Reva had sensed his stare, she whipped around to face him. "Finally. I thought you would sleep all day."

"Maybe if I'd gotten any sleep last night," he said with a sly grin. "Come here."

Reva inched toward him, too slowly for his liking, so he grabbed her arm and tugged her down. She landed on him with an *oof*, her breasts pressed against his chest. Crow's heart swelled at her nearness. He tugged a lock of her hair behind her ear and sighed silently. It had been so long since he'd held his wife, and for a little while, he had wondered if he ever would again. He swept forward and kissed her, his lips caressing hers.

Reva relaxed against him, returning the kiss, but only for a moment. "All right," she murmured, brushing his cheek before pushing herself up. "I need to find my corset and shirt, then we need to get out of here."

"I'm sure we have a *few* minutes," Crow complained at the loss of her warmth.

"When has anything only lasted a few minutes with you? A-ha!" She swiped her clothing off the floor near his head.

"Are you sure you need to put it back on? I wouldn't mind," he said with a wink.

"You're insufferable." She smirked and tugged the rest of her clothing on. "Get dressed. The stalks have moved, and we're losing daylight. I don't want to get stuck in the cornfield without shelter."

The thought of another night in his personal hell sent a shiver through him. He threw on his clothes quickly and shouldered his pack. Under other circumstances, he might've insisted they eat first, but he doubted he would be able to keep a single bite down.

"Ready?" Reva asked.

Crow paused and stared out the windows—clear of any stalks. Which meant only one thing... "A new scarecrow is waiting out there."

"Let's hope this one is planted to the post," Reva muttered.

She inhaled deeply and ripped the door inward. Crow followed her from the shed, trying desperately not to look at his old post. But he couldn't stop his eyes from straying.

A new scarecrow hung there without the slightest movement. The male had bright red hair, elven ears, and an expression of frozen horror. His ragged knit clothing drooped over his too-thin frame. It appeared to be mere fabric stuffed with straw at first glance, but the muffled sobs were undeniably real. It tore at Crow's already fragile state-of-mind. That had been him ten years ago. He hadn't been as lucky as the Baobhan sith who had somehow managed to break free of the post. Took *his* place. Every blazing hot ray of sunlight would land on him, every rain cloud or sheet of ice that fell from the sky. And he would *feel* it.

There was no way they could help the unfortunate fae, however. Not right then. It would take too long to discover how to break his personal curse. Even if they were able to, another soul would appear tomorrow if Locasta remained living.

"When we're finished with Locasta, we'll come back," Crow said as much to himself as to Reva. He would want to make sure killing her released the field.

Reva wove her fingers between his and squeezed. "Let's get you out of here."

Crow nodded and took off at a near run. He wanted *out* of there and every moment mattered. His mind buzzed. It was as if the field was trying to erase his thoughts again, but he kept hyper-focused on the feel of Reva's hand in his. She grounded him. Anchored him to reality. He could still taste her on his lips. Phantom touches lingered where she had caressed his skin the night before, leaving his entire body sensitive to the smallest breeze.

They plowed through the stalks all the morning and into the afternoon without a break. He tried to see nothing except the path directly before him, but glimpses of white bones caught his peripheral more than once. When they did finally stop, it was only to dig through their packs for food before continuing. The food taken from the shed was flavorless now that it was out of the building, but it still filled their stomachs.

Finally, as twilight touched the sky, turning it deep pink, they emerged from the cornfield. Crow sucked in a deep breath the moment his boots hit green grass. The stench of the field had nearly gagged him, but he didn't care. They were out. The field was behind them. On their journey back from the North, they would take an entirely different route.

After another few staggering steps, Crow fell to his knees

and closed his eyes. His body quivered with exhaustion, his mind reveling at being free. He could still feel the maliciousness of the field's curse deep in his marrow. It wanted to reclaim him—wanted him to stay. Almost demanded it. But he would never willingly allow himself to be its prisoner again.

Reva's footsteps came to a halt in front of him and he reached out to her without opening his eyes. His arms wrapped around her waist and he buried his face in her abdomen.

Her fingers combed gently through his hair for a few minutes, comforting him, before she tipped his head back to look at her. "It's behind us," she said. "We keep going."

Keep going. She was right—the only thing they could do was move forward—and the farther they went, the better he was sure to feel. Crow nodded and climbed to his feet. Beyond them rose the Gnome King's mountain. A red haze hovered over the top of the rocky peak. Years of fae travel to and from the Gnome City had worn a path to the base. Tunnels ran through the interior of the rocky cliffs and eventually came out at a clearing surrounded by the mountain walls. That was where the gnomes had created their city, but the tunnels were where they kept their valuables. Crow knew because he'd searched them years ago, carefully mapping them out as he went, in an attempt to find the stone. This time, he planned to be less covert.

"Would you rather climb the cliff or go through the pass?" he asked.

Reva chewed her bottom lip as they walked. "I think that depends on how we want to approach the king."

"If we confront him in front of his subjects, he may kill us on the spot to maintain his image."

She tapped a finger on her chin as she seemed to mull it over. "So we sneak in and corner him when he's alone. I don't suppose you know where his private chambers are?"

"How would I know that?" Crow asked with a mischievous tone. When she shrugged, he slipped his pack to one shoulder and pulled out the folded paper, hidden in the seams of his pack.

He held it out to her. "I do, actually."

Reva slowly unfolded the map and a smile crept over her face. "Well, aren't you full of surprises?"

"I told you that I've been inside a few times." He inched closer, so his shoulder rubbed against hers. The light scent of vanilla mixed with spices had his blood pumping faster. He pointed to an area at the top left of the map and forced himself to focus. "We scale the cliff and enter here. It's the closest entrance to his rooms."

"*I'll* scale the cliff." Reva handed him back the paper, and he tucked it into his pants pocket. "You should scout ahead."

Crow opened his mouth to say he wasn't any faster at climbing than she was when she smiled. *His wings.* They were healed. He could *fly* again. His bird form seemed to wrestle for control of his body, eager to take flight, but he couldn't leave her yet. There was still a half day's walk ahead of them. "Deal," he said, feeling lighter than he had in years.

Each minute of their walk was like ten. Crow knew he was going to fly when they reached their destination and it drove him mad to wait. But Reva did her best to distract him by chatting about Ozma. He tried very hard to stay engaged in the conversation, but it was difficult to care about Mombi and Oz being villainous in that moment when the sky was so bright. Mombi had always been rumored to be bizarre and Oz was a faerie fruit-addicted bastard. It wasn't all that surprising that they had joined forces to banish the true heir to the Land of Oz into the dark place. Once Locasta was dealt with, they would meet Ozma in the Emerald City. If Mombi and Oz were still alive then, they would decide how to change that.

When Crow and Reva reached the base of the mountain far from the tunnel entrance, he shifted anxiously from one foot to the other. The incline was steep but manageable. There were plenty of footholds along the gray stone. Smooth white rock peeked out from the dark gray limestone, offering Reva plenty of places to grab. Still, unease blossomed in his chest with her climbing on her own.

"Are you sure you're okay with this climb?"

Reva raised an eyebrow. "Is that a legitimate question?"

A vision of Reva scaling an even steeper mountainside surfaced in his mind. They'd been fleeing the West, seeking a haven from Locasta's wrath. The edge of the cliff had crumbled, and they'd fallen twenty feet to a wide ledge. It was either climb the cliff to safety, or edge along the ridge and hope it led somewhere worth going. Reva hadn't thought twice before launching herself up the stone wall.

"I'll be around if you get stuck," he said.

She scoffed. "I won't."

Unable to wait any longer, Crow willed his bird form forward. One moment, he stood beside Reva, the next he flexed his wings as wide as they could go. The muscles strained, shaky from lack of use, but he still felt powerful. He hopped once, twice, three times, testing out his now-mended body. He gave Reva a caw and launched into the air.

He gained height, then lost it. His body remembered how to fly, but it had been so long that it took a few extra moments for him to find the rhythm. Once he did, his heart soared higher than his wings could ever hope to carry him. The wind rushed over his feathers, welcoming him back.

Reva was only a few feet off the ground when he let himself drop. He swooped down just above her head and snapped his wings wide. They caught the air, carrying him upward again. "Behave," Reva shouted after him. His chuckle came out as a breathy *caw*.

But now that he'd given himself a moment of joy, there was a job to be done. He flew to the top of the cliff, a yard below the red mist. A bare, twisted tree offered the perfect perch. He landed on the sturdiest branch and squinted into the clearing below.

The stone buildings were so minuscule from this vantage point that they looked like children's playthings. Stone dots—the gnomes themselves—moved about like ants. There didn't seem to be any scouts where Crow perched, waiting, but he would stay put just to be sure they weren't making rounds.

Every few minutes, he sailed off the tree to check on Reva's whereabouts. She was making slow, but steady, progress and was nearly to an oval ledge large enough for her to take a break. He settled back on the branch and scoured the round entrances carved into the stone mountain, each leading to a portion of the tunnels. No guards. No civilians. It seemed as if all the gnomes were busy in the clearing or hidden inside, but that didn't seem right. There had always been at least a handful of guards when he'd snuck in. His talons clicked on the tree as he paced along the branch. Something was wrong. He needed to get to Reva.

Crow leapt into the air and plunged toward where she was. Where she *should've* been. But the cliffside was empty. He tucked his wings against his sides, and the wind whizzed over him. A panicked screech left his throat. Reva hadn't fallen—there wasn't a body on the ground below—but a spark of green leaked from inside a hidden tunnel entrance.

Shit.

Crow transformed into his fae form again before he hit the rocky ledge. He landed on his feet, dark hair falling in his face, and strode into the tunnel with blades at the ready. Another blast of green drew him farther into the tunnel entrance.

Crow found Reva around the first turn with two dozen gnomes surrounding her. They were varying shades and textures of stone—smooth obsidian, beige pockmarked felsite, tan dolomite covered in clear crystals, and striped sandstone—but all of them only came up to her shoulders. Their naked stone bodies had a vaguely elven shape, but their bulbous heads and severe underbites were uniquely *gnome*.

While the gnomes weren't what Crow would consider intimidating creatures, the iron spears they had pointed at Reva's chest were another story. Every blast of Reva's magic that slammed into their stone bodies only served to push them back.

For each round gnome that retreated a step, another took its place.

Crow swept his blades across the nearest guard. White lines scarred the stone fae, who whirled on him. Sharp pain stabbed him between the shoulder blades at the same time the scarred gnome leveled his spear at Crow's chest.

"Stop," Reva shouted.

"Surrender your weapons," one of the guards said, his voice like gravel. "You," he said to another guard, "bind her hands behind her back."

Crow tensed, ready to leap to his wife's defense, but she shook her head. She allowed one gnome to take her pack before her hands were tugged behind her, and she stayed utterly still as they shackled her with stone manacles. He sighed and retracted his blades. The gnomes quickly unbuckled his bracers, ripped away his pack, then ran their stone hands over his body in search of other weapons. Crow held Reva's gaze the entire time, hoping they would miss the knife in his boot.

They didn't.

But they didn't search Reva. He suppressed a grin, remembering how she'd used his other knife to clean her nails the night before they entered the cornfield and she'd never returned it.

"Move," a gnome ordered, shoving the tip of his spear into Crow's side.

Crow released a long breath and allowed himself to be led deeper into the tunnels. He memorized each turn they made to add it to his map later when they escaped. *With* the stone. There was no leaving without it. Not when facing Locasta empty-handed would undoubtedly end with both him and Reva cursed again. And Crow knew the Northern Witch well enough to understand there would be no breaking her curses a second time.

CHAPTER EIGHTEEN

REVA

"You mother-fuckers!" Reva seethed as the gnomes shoved her forward with the tips of their iron spears. The gnomes each had the same basic shape, their height reaching to her shoulders, their upper backs hunched, lower jaw set forward, and not a drop of cloth clung to their hardened bodies. Several of the gnomes' stony outer layers were full of large and small holes splattering their entire lengths, while others were as smooth as a newborn elf's skin. Each one varied in color. Some obsidian, others topaz, crystal, and so on. She'd never seen the Gnome King before, had only heard about him from other fae, but she wondered which of the gnomes he most resembled.

Crow's eyes locked on hers, and his expression told her to play along. They were outnumbered, her magic wasn't doing a drop of damage to them, and one gnome's spear was aimed right at Crow's heart. The gnomes didn't need to lock stone manacles on her wrists or try to attack her with their spears. They could have played nice themselves, but they hadn't. However, she needed to cooperate for the time being.

Another sharp jab came at Reva's back. She cursed under her breath but followed the gnomes as they led the way toward a narrow opening within the cave.

Inside, the tunnel opened into a wider space and a long strip of pale blue fire along the wall lit their way. Below the flames, trickles of water flowed down to the pebbled floor, creating puddles. An earthy smell surrounded her that wasn't at all unpleasant, almost intoxicating—the *only* thing that wasn't offensive here.

The tunnel led to a junction with three other oval openings. Gnomes seemed to appear out of nowhere as they pushed themselves out from the walls. These gnomes, made of limestone, took over for the others and shoved Reva and Crow down the tunnel.

"How much farther?" Crow asked.

"Remain silent or we eat your flesh," a gnome with half his face crumbled away bellowed.

Crow's jaw clenched, and Reva could tell he was trying desperately to hold his tongue.

The gnomes took them down two more flame-lit tunnels, the walls jagged and sharp, with protruding granite thorns. At the end of the tunnel was a whirling stone staircase leading down into the area below. Reva held her breath steady while taking the first step. She stared at the back of Crow's head, hoping nothing would come out of the shadows to cause him harm.

Once she descended the last step into a large room with sparkling quartz floors, she'd expected the Gnome King to be waiting on a stone throne, but he wasn't. There was no throne at all. In fact, the room was completely bare except for the twinkling gemstones that were worked into the stone walls. Sapphires, amethysts, diamonds, opals, and others she couldn't name.

On the other side of the room, a door creaked open, one that she wouldn't have noticed since it had blended in with the wall. Out stepped a looming figure, taller and more muscular than

Crow. His hard, smooth outer layer was the color of ivory, and each muscle in his chest appeared chiseled to perfection. Midnight blue hair hung straight down to his waist in silken sheets and tucked behind his pointed ears. The male fae didn't much resemble the gnomes who still held her and Crow hostage, aside from being made of stone. Her gaze widened as it roamed to the area between his legs, which was on full display. Even his stone cock was practically a work of art.

The male bared his teeth into a smile, causing his high cheekbones to appear even higher. It was as if he'd been sculpted by beauty itself.

"Why are you here in my palace, maiden?" His voice came out stern.

So, this was the Gnome King. When maidens ventured here to try and make him fall in love, she wondered if any had thought about how it would feel to fuck a stone cock. It certainly didn't look like it would be comfortable, regardless of how good it might look.

The Gnome King's cobalt eyes drifted to Crow and hardened. "You dare to bring a male with you?"

You mean, I brought her, Crow mouthed to Reva.

Reva took a breath, trying to keep calm when all she wanted were the manacles to be removed from her wrists. "Gnome King—"

"You may call me Ceres," he interrupted.

"Ceres," Reva said slowly, "we need your help. Locasta is attempting to take over Oz, no matter who she ruins in the process."

"Why should I care who rules Oz?" Ceres shrugged and folded his arms over his muscular chest.

"Because you live here," Reva spat.

"No one can defeat me here." Ceres dropped his arms and moved to her in three quick strides. He lifted her chin between his cool fingertips. "Maiden, aren't you here because you think you can make me love again? That is why they all come."

Reva knew Crow was carefully watching, ready to intervene if he needed to.

"I'm not here for that. I couldn't give a fuck if you fall in love again or not." She paused, reeling her emotions back in. "I'm sorry. You've lost someone important to you. I understand. But that doesn't mean you should destroy every female who walks into your kingdom."

"Who do you think you are?" The Gnome King leaned his face closer to hers, his breath hitting her cheek. She held back a shiver from the coldness.

"We've never met before, but I know you've heard of me. I'm Reva."

Ceres's hand lowered from her chin as his eyes narrowed, recognition setting in. "Reva. The once-ruler of the West?"

Reva slowly nodded, keeping her eyes trained on his. She didn't look at her husband because she didn't want the Gnome King to see how much she cared for Crow. That could lead to torture, which was already highly likely.

"Locasta had placed a curse on me out of spite, then turned me into the monstrous Wicked Witch of the West." Even then she couldn't help but remember her taloned fingers, her green skin, the pustules, the need and desire to hunt, to kill, to torment.

Ceres's tongue scraped the inside of his cheek, the sound echoing. "I don't believe it. Dorothy killed the ruler of the West. She's dead."

There was only one way to show him, but with the iron poking at her flesh, she couldn't conjure the magic. "Remove my manacles and I'll demonstrate."

"She did have green powers outside," one of the gnomes hissed, his shoulders growing rigid.

Ceres tapped the side of his stone cheek. Reva guessed he was weighing his options—murder them there or let her prove herself. She wouldn't make it easy to kill them if that was what he chose.

"Free her," he finally said. His gaze shifted to Crow, his

145

white eyelashes lowering. "But not him."

Reva held her breath. She had to remember if anyone tried to torture Crow down here, he could transform and save himself. But she knew he wouldn't leave her, no matter how much she would shout at him to do so.

A gnome shuffled behind her and unlocked her manacles. Reva rubbed at her wrists—they were sore and red from her yanking at them.

Stepping toward the Gnome King and taking a deep breath, she let the power crackle and churn inside her until the magic pulsed green on her palm, like emerald lightning flashing inside a darkened cloud. "If you want me to continue, I can strike the ground and make thunder rattle your walls."

"Stop," Ceres demanded, not removing his gaze from her hand.

Her magic ceased, the emerald color disappearing from sight. "Now"—Reva cocked her head and smiled—"I may not be able to end you or your gnomes' lives at the moment, but I can destroy your entire palace before you could ever end me."

Crow inhaled sharply in a way that told her to watch it. She ignored him.

"Will you help us defeat Locasta?" she asked, taking a backward step closer to Crow.

Ceres studied her, stretching the time out. "I need to think about it. First, I'll have to figure out what I want in return."

Reva held back a shake of the head. What all kings and queens seemed to want was more territory. "I can give you more land once I reclaim what's mine. All the land near the deserts."

He scanned her up and down, licking his lips. "I'm not sure more land is what I want, *Reva*. We'll discuss this more in the morning." His gaze shifted to one of the crystal gnomes. "Take them to a guest room for now."

The Gnome King turned away, but glanced one more time at her over his shoulder before sauntering through the same secret door that he'd used to enter. Reva turned to Crow, who was focused on her, the vein in his jaw ticking.

"Come on," a gnome grunted, removing Crow's manacles. He then waved at them to follow him back up the stairs. No iron spear this time.

"I don't like the way he's watching you," Crow whispered in her ear. He was jealous, but there was nothing to worry about. She wasn't wooed by males who slit the throats of their females.

"It's nothing," she said quietly. "I'll bet Ceres looks at any maiden that way before he slaughters them."

"We're calling him Ceres now?"

Reva rolled her eyes. "Just remember what I told you yesterday. You know, in the shed?"

A side-smile formed on Crow's face and he pressed a hand to his chest, letting her know that he loved her too.

Neither one said anything else as they reached the top of the stairs and followed the crystal gnome. Once they reached the end of the tunnel, the other gnomes stayed at their posts while the crystal one continued to lead them down several tunnels. There was an elaborate crisscrossing arched design above them made from rose quartz, and protruding jagged stone poked out from the walls. An imaginary wind appeared to blow against the blue flames highlighting their way. The only sounds were the stomp of the gnome's feet and his heavy breathing.

The gnome turned the corner and stopped in front of what looked to be stone bars. He pulled open the door and ushered them in.

Reva and Crow stepped inside, and she wondered where their packs had been taken. He shut the caged door behind them, locking it. So much for *guest* room.

"If you're thirsty there's water over there." The gnome pointed in between the bars to the far corner, where water trickled into a large garnet bucket, before turning to walk away.

In the middle of the room was a rectangular stone that must have been the bed. Crow took a seat in the center of it. "We got farther than I expected. And you're still alive."

Reva sank down beside him. "And you weren't tortured."

"Not yet." He rubbed at a red spot on his arm where one of the gnomes had poked him too hard with the iron. "He's going to try something, Reva. I hated the way he looked at you."

"Let him look." She stared at the granite flooring. "The problem now is we're locked in a stone cage. I was expecting a room that we could sneak out of."

He winked at her, his smile lighting up his face. "You still underestimate me, my love."

It took her a moment to realize what he was implying. He could shift. "Oh, *oh*!" She smirked. "If we had time and we weren't here, I would kiss you all over."

"I'll take on the mouth for now." He leaned forward, stealing a quick kiss from her that tingled all the way down to her toes.

She then whispered in his ear, "I'll tell you when to go." Quietly, she slipped the knife from her boot and set it into his palm.

CHAPTER NINETEEN

CROW

Reva pressed Crow's knife into his hand. He winked at her as he tucked the blade into his boot, though he wasn't sure how much use it would be against stone. Still, it was better than nothing. "I'll be quick," he promised. Then he called forth his other form. One moment he stood six inches taller than his wife—the next, a black cloud exploded around him and he became a bird in the time it would take to snap his fingers.

Leaving Reva alone made Crow's insides squirm. The Gnome King could beat her to death, or drag her to a pit for a slow demise, or simply crush her with his bare hands. But they still needed to go through with their plan to get the red stone. Only, now they also needed a second plan to escape. Neither could be accomplished from inside a cell, so he gave her the softest of caws and, on her signal, slipped through the bars.

He hopped down the hallway, retracing their steps with the help of the enchanted blue flames that ran along the walls, until he found what looked to be an abandoned, dead-end tunnel. Cobwebs hung from the ceiling and a crack in the stone let in a trickle of water, leaving the floor slick with mildew. This was a safe enough place.

When Crow was broken, changing back and forth between his forms had taken every ounce of energy he had. Bones either had to break or mend accordingly and it never failed to steal his breath away. But now, he shut his eyes and willed himself back into fae form as effortlessly as blinking. His clothes were just as he left them, his hair only slightly mussed.

Crow stayed hunched near the entrance and pulled the map from his pocket. He hadn't charted this part, but he was sure he wasn't far off from tunnels he *had* explored. Hopefully something would begin to look familiar on the map sooner rather than later. The dripping water was likely from the hot spring on the lower mountain ledge. There were a few areas with vegetation, but only one with a spring, which told him two things: they were being kept in the lower tunnels—perhaps even below ground—and they were on the east side of the city.

Crow studied the map, committing to memorize the most likely tunnels that this one connected to, before creeping out into the main halls. He was light on his feet as he explored, ducking in and out of small alcoves when the sound of stomping stone feet neared. A handful of gnomes passed, laughing and joking in Gnomish. Once the danger was gone, he continued on, all the while recording the turns in his mind. Left, right, right, left, right.

The tunnels seemed to stretch on forever before he caught his bearings. Each new passage looked just like the last, with blue flames and smoothly carved walls. The ceilings were left rough, as if to add character, and were the only thing that gave any hint of his location. A small x marked the top of a particular tunnel, so well-blended with the cracks that it was impossible to see if one wasn't looking for it. Crow, however, had been the one to score the stone when he'd explored last time. He quickly unfolded the yellow map, the creases wearing thin, and found the corresponding x marking which tunnel began there. Later, when he returned to Reva, he would draw the tunnels it had taken to reach that place and score another symbol on the ceiling in front of the cell.

"All right," he whispered to himself. "This way."

Based on his markings, behind him lay the cells, and before him, nothing of value in regard to the stone. He was surprisingly close to the king's chambers. Only such an arrogant king would allow prisoners to be kept so near his own rooms. The tunnels were a maze to navigate, but Crow couldn't have been the only one to ever scout them.

With a quick glance at the map, Crow planned his route, but there was no telling how much time he had before the gnomes returned to the cell. He didn't want them to find Reva alone, so he would go back to her and then leave again after the guards checked on them.

"Did you send the message?" a familiar, deep, gravelly voice bellowed ahead of him—the Gnome King.

Crow bolted back to the last hiding place he'd seen, and without a moment to spare. Two sets of heavy footsteps trudged toward him.

"I did, Your Majesty.'"

"Wonderful. Locasta will surely reward us with more than a simple promise of land at some point in the future," the king huffed. "And land near the desert at that! As if we hadn't relocated for a reason."

"The Good Witch of the North will be generous, I'm sure," the other gnome agreed. "Especially given who the male is."

The king laughed heartily. "He probably thinks I didn't recognize him—the fool. What sort of help do you suspect they were going to ask from me?"

"We can only guess, sire."

"I think I'll do more than that," the king said. Their footsteps stopped just past Crow's hiding place, and his heart hammered in his chest. "Bring me the female tomorrow. We'll have lunch together in my chambers—alone. I'll get her to tell me everything."

151

"So you *don't* want us to prepare the blade or the hammer?" the gnome asked, confused.

"Not quite yet."

"Of course."

The footsteps sounded again, this time going in two different directions. Crow waited until he could no longer hear them and transformed into his bird form, flying back to Reva as fast as his wings could carry him. His small body slipped through the bars and he landed on Reva's shoulder with rumpled feathers.

"What's wrong?" she asked, seeming to sense all was not well.

Crow's beak opened as he tried to slow his rapid breathing. He was too wound up to shift—his body tense and his mind frantic, unlike the hyper-focused anger he'd felt entering the tunnels to save Reva. Still, he had to warn her that Locasta knew they were in Gnome City.

He hopped off Reva's shoulder and glided to the stone bed. There was nothing to write with inside the cell so he would have to do his best without language. He lifted a small piece of crumbled rock in his beak and puffed his chest.

Reva blinked at him in confusion. "A big rock?" she ventured.

In a way... Crow strutted around in a circle with his wings out.

"A gnome?"

Crow hopped in excitement, but he needed her to know it was the king. Flapping his wings, he landed on her head and set the piece of rock down, then hopped down again and cawed as if he were unequaled.

"Hat? No! Crown! The Gnome King!"

Crow flapped his wings and began delivering her small rocks from around the room.

"I have no idea," Reva said with a scowl. "Pile?"

Crow shook his head.

"The Gnome King smashed another gnome into pieces?"

152

Crow sighed. This was impossible. How else could he show *delivered?*

"Spell it out with these," Reva suggested, poking at the pile of pebbles.

Crow hadn't thought of that. He arranged the small stones into elvish letters. Finally, he'd spelled out *sent message to L.* He'd run out of stones to spell the rest, but Reva would know who he meant.

"The Gnome King sent Locasta a message?" Reva's eyes were wide and burning with unfiltered fury. "About us?"

Crow cawed.

"That son of a bitch! I'm going to turn him into rubble!"

Crow flicked at a rock with his beak. They still needed the stone.

"Yes, yes," she murmured. "The stone first, if we can find it."

Crow's body shuddered with exhaustion. He didn't have the energy to tell her his theory on the location of the stone, and there was the more pressing issue of the king wanting her to have lunch with him. He moved the pebbles to spell out *you lunch alone king.*

Reva's brows rose up her forehead. "The king wants me to have lunch with him alone? Why?" she mused, more to herself than him. She sat down beside him and lifted him into her lap. "Actually, this may work in our favor. I'll distract him while you keep looking for the stone. If he doesn't agree to give it to us, we'll steal it."

Crow wanted to tell her what a horrible idea that was. The Gnome King was far from stupid and, given that he killed every female who dared enter his city, also extremely dangerous. But Reva knew that and still wanted to go through with this, and Crow knew better than to tell her otherwise. So, he settled into her warm lap to relax enough to transform. It didn't help that he was no longer used to exerting so much energy to switch between forms. With an agitated huff, he ruffled his feathers and

153

counted backward from a hundred to help calm his nerves.

CHAPTER TWENTY

REVA

It had taken a while for Crow to shift back to his male form the night before, but he'd finally transformed after multiple tries. As he straightened on the stone bed, Reva watched as beads of perspiration dripped down his forehead and neck. His skin even appeared paler. Neither one had gotten any sleep and they'd only had water, that had a strange taste, from the bucket.

"Will you be able to shift today?" Reva asked, her lips thinning as she continued to study him. "Perhaps you shouldn't try again. I'll just get the information from Ceres myself, then we can find the stone together."

He rubbed at his chin and arched a dark eyebrow. "There's nothing wrong with my shifting—I'm only wound up. I don't like this. Since Locasta knows we're here, who knows what will happen?"

Ceres just *had* to reveal to Reva's enemy that she was still alive. Now their plans would have to be altered.

"She won't come." Reva shook her head. "I know her well enough, and she hates to chance defeat, so she won't show herself—yet. Her minions will be the ones sent to do the dirty work." When Thelia was born it had been different because Locasta knew she could defeat Reva in an exhausted state. And once she'd been in the Northern Witch's control, Reva had been released into the wild, only secretly meeting when Locasta wanted to make her dance for her, or slap her across the face.

"And if she *does* decide to come?" Crow inched closer to Reva, brushing his fingers against hers. "Then what? I know her well too, and it won't be good."

"Then she comes." Reva grasped his hand and gave it a quick squeeze before letting go. "We fight."

"The gnomes are tricky to take down."

"That they are." She paused. "I didn't try for long, though. And I figured I should play nice, or *nicer*, so we could find the stone."

"There has to be a way to track it down." Crow chewed on his lip.

"If something was that important, most fae would keep it on themselves at all times." She would.

"He's naked, Reva." Crow cocked his head. "Unless you think he stuck it up his asshole."

"Now that, my dear Crow, could very well be the case." Reva laughed and covered her mouth. He was right. There wasn't a single stone or jewel clinging to Ceres's body. No rings, no necklaces, no bracelets. Nothing. Not even a crown.

He started to smile too, dipping his head toward hers. But then a clatter and heavy footsteps sounded from outside their cell and down the tunnel. Reva and Crow broke apart and watched as two gnomes stopped in front of their barred cell. Neither were the same gnomes from earlier. One was dark magenta with silver stripes across her belly and the other was entirely translucent with a hazy sheen.

"The Gnome King requests the female's company for lunch," the magenta one said, eyeing Reva and pointing a staff at her.

"A request can be denied," Reva answered, trying to make it seem as though she wasn't anxious to attend.

"Go or die." The clear gnome shrugged. "That's your choice."

"Well, then, with that sort of *hospitality*, I might as well attend." Reva stood from the bed and didn't look back at Crow as she stepped toward the door. It made a scratching noise as the magenta gnome pulled it open.

Crow had tried to return the knife to Reva, but she'd snuck it back on him, figuring he would need it more than her. It would be better than no weapon at all. At the very least, they could scrape it across the gnomes' eyes.

Reva exited the cell and followed the two gnomes down the jagged-stone tunnel. She knew as soon as the coast was clear that Crow would transform into his bird form—if he could muster up the strength.

The earthy scent of sandalwood from the stone itself enveloped her, stronger here than in the cell. Liquid dripped from the ceiling, a couple of droplets pelting her skin. The blue flames guided their way, the tunnels remaining silent as they walked down them and descended the stairs to the empty room where she'd first met Ceres. If this were meant to be where they were to eat, she wondered if they would be dining on the floor. As if answering her thoughts, the hidden door, from where the Gnome King had first appeared, opened in the wall with a soft groan.

The two guards waved their spears for her to follow them. Once she crossed into the new room, her gaze landed on the wall. It was covered in sparkling blue jewels, matching the color of Ceres's hair. Standing before them in a neat row were dozens of pale skeletons wearing blood-stained gowns. There was at least one dress of every color, all made of the finest materials, and ranging in size from pixie to troll.

Reva inhaled sharply, at a loss for words over the collection of the dead before her.

"These are the remains of the females who thought they could sway me," a deep voice rumbled.

Reva's gaze settled, unnerved, on the long rectangular table in the middle of the room, leading up to Ceres. He sat regally in his chair with one leg propped over the other. "I see," she said. "I'm glad I didn't wear a gown then."

His cobalt eyes glittered with amusement as he watched every move she made on her way to the table. "You may sit across from me."

Strewn along the table were different rocks resting on stone plates, smooth in texture—gray, white, and brown in color. This must be their lunch... She believed him to be toying with her. Only a fool would believe she'd eat rocks.

"I have a better idea," Reva purred, sauntering toward him instead, and running her fingertips over the rocks.

He narrowed his eyes at her as she plopped down on the edge of the table in front of him.

"And what idea is that?" Ceres lifted his hand and drew a light line with his fingernail across her throat. "For me to bleed you out right here? It would add to the flavor of dinner."

Reva didn't let any fear show as she spread her legs apart. "We both know if you wanted me dead, I already would be." She unbuttoned the outer layer of her tunic, exposing the corset and curves of the tops of her breasts beneath. "How many of the maidens did you fuck before you killed them?"

With quick motions, he grabbed her from the table and set her on his lap, her legs open and cradling his. "How many do you think?"

"Too many." She could feel the hardness and twitch of his cock beneath her. She tried not to let the disgust show in her face as she leaned forward, pushing her breasts against his hard chest.

"The maidens—their *softness*—disgusts me. But I'll take the momentary pleasure anyway, then after I get my fuck, I remove their soft skin so only hard bone is left." He ran his hand up her face, through Reva's hair, and yanked her head back. "If my wife

158

couldn't live, then why should any females be allowed to? Outside of my gnomes, of course."

Reva maintained a neutral expression, but she couldn't control the rapid beat of her heart. In that moment, she wanted to chip away at his hard skin, the way he'd done to those innocent females. Even though they'd known what he was capable of before trying to come and win his affection. "Do *I* disgust you?" she asked slowly.

Ceres released her hair, his gaze roaming over her as he ground his teeth together. "I'm intrigued by your power and more so by how much you've suffered. While your body is soft, your spirit is not. If you were to be my new queen, we would be unstoppable."

This mad king had just talked about slitting her throat and now he was talking about her becoming his queen? Reva thought about what he'd done to Tin's mother, how he had ruined an innocent child, even though he hadn't known she was pregnant. But, had he known the condition Tin's mother was in, Reva doubted it would have stopped him.

She pressed her forehead against his, pretending that it were Crow she was talking to, so she could sound sincere. "If I become your wife, will you give me the stone to defeat Locasta?"

"So, that's why you came here. For the stone." His vicious smile spread. "If you agree to be my wife, your body will become hard like mine, and only then might I relay the secret to you. Depending on how well you obey me first."

The door burst open, and Reva jumped at the loud bang. Ceres remained still as though he'd expected the gnome to enter all along. In walked the same crystal gnome who had originally taken them to their cell, but he wasn't alone—he held a stone bird cage.

Reva gasped at what—*who*—stirred inside, cawing in rage. Crow.

Gritting her teeth, Reva hopped from Ceres's lap. He stretched his hand forward and gripped her wrist before she could leave, squeezing tight.

"You think I didn't recognize him?" Ceres boomed. "Locasta had warned me that he may one day come, and described to me exactly what he looked like. She believed *you* were dead, however. But now she knows you're alive, and I know you love *him*. The only way you can be my queen is if he's dead. Locasta wants him for her own, but that would prevent me from getting what I want. You would never stop searching for him."

"No," Reva said with force.

"I think he will be a fantastic dessert. Don't you think? You aren't yet able to eat stone, so now I have something to force down your throat." The king threw his head back and laughed, the sound bouncing off the walls.

Reva couldn't help the horrified expression that she knew crossed her face, imagining him stuffing her throat with Crow's bloody meat. She spat at the Gnome King's feet. "Never."

"Guards!" Ceres growled. "Fire up the flames and cook the bird. Do it while he's alive."

"No!" Reva screamed, thrashing and trying to escape the grasp that Ceres had on her wrist. Nothing she did loosened his hand.

The gnome did as he was told, carrying the cage back toward the door.

Anger pulsed through Reva. Uncontrollable desperation and fury. "I said *no!*" The magic in her veins danced with furor, harder than ever, rattling the walls.

"You can shake the palace all you want," Ceres cooed, releasing her wrists. "I failed to mention before that whatever falls down here rebuilds itself."

Lightning rippled over Reva, not affecting the king in the slightest. She thought about Thelia and how her daughter's magic had split Glinda's palace in half. That was only a taste of what Thelia would be able to do one day. Reva knew—because her daughter had inherited that power from *her*. Rattling the mountain was just a hint of what Reva could do if she put her all

160

into this moment.

Her magic shot toward the guard holding Crow's cage and knocked him on his ass. The guard's jaw opened, seeming stunned as he got back up, leaving the cage on the ground.

"You're just wasting time," Ceres said with a smirk.

"You forget what storms can bring." Reva whirled around to face Ceres. "There can be tornadoes, there can be hurricanes, there can be floods, there can be earthquakes." She'd never had to use this amount of power, didn't know if she truly could. The thunder roared around her, causing fragments of the ceiling to fall.

"I told you"—Ceres crossed his arms—"it will rebuild itself and I'll survive. But you'll kill yourself and your precious *Crow*. Your undying love for each other won't save you."

The gnome guard lunged toward her and Reva roared, the quaking from her magic pushing into him, crumbling his body to pieces. Not giving Ceres time to make a move, Reva barreled forward, shoving her hands against the Gnome King's chest, and slamming him into the wall.

Reva felt him struggling to move, but the lightning held him in place. He stood frozen, like the statue he should have always been. Reva held her concentration, making his body shake from the inside out. A jagged line shot up his middle all the way to his scalp, splitting his face in half. He wasn't able to scream aloud but she knew he was screaming inside himself.

His entire body slowly separated, cracks covering every inch of him until he burst into hundreds of pieces, scattering to the floor. Dust filled the air.

"Rebuild *that*, asshole." Reva coughed, taking a step back. She reeled her magic in, her body still shaking. Red light reflected all over the walls of the room. Bright, so bright. Never before had she seen a red so vivid. Her gaze landed on the source—a heart-shaped stone laying in the rubble that was once the Gnome King. The stone they needed had been *inside* the Gnome King and now that she held it—his heart—he was no more. Was this what Tin's stone heart had looked like before Thelia had freed it?

Crow cawed from his cage behind her, and she quickly scooped up the red stone.

Reva cradled her prize and hurried toward Crow. She opened the cage, reached in with her free hand, and pulled him up toward her. "Are you all right?"

He nodded.

Her muscles relaxed and she placed him on her shoulder. "Don't shift. Not now. It will be harder for them to detect one fae."

As she buttoned up her tunic, the door flew open again—gnome guard after gnome guard stood there, all holding their spears. None of them moved as they stared at the crumbled pieces of the king on the floor.

"Looks like I'm your queen now," Reva said, holding up the stone heart. "If you want to remain whole, then I suggest you help me."

"They're almost here," one of the gnomes covered with emeralds said as he broke from the group.

"Who?" Reva asked. "Locasta or her night beasts?"

"No," another rasped, "she sent something worse."

"Here's the plan," she said. "Assemble your archers, lock down the city, barricade any doors. After you've defeated this threat, march your forces to the Emerald City and help liberate it. Do what I've instructed, and you may come home and be free. I will leave you in peace as long as no other maidens are murdered, understand?" That seemed a fair bargain to her.

"Yes, my queen," the gnomes answered in unison.

"Good. Now that that's settled..." Deafening booms came from above and outside the stone palace. Reva sighed, staring up at the ceiling. "Fuck, can anything go right?"

162

CHAPTER TWENTY-ONE

CROW

*W*orse. What could possibly be worse than Locasta and the cursed pixies?

Crow quickly transformed back into his fae form and watched as the gnomes followed the orders Reva had given. Spears in hand, the stone fae stormed into the tunnels, shouting directions at other gnomes to get to the top tunnels. He exchanged a worried glance with Reva. "Our packs?"

"You," Reva barked to the last gnome still inside the dead king's secret room. "Get our belongings."

The gray-stoned gnome backtracked through a second hidden door without a peep and returned, only moments later, with both Crow and Reva's bags. He held them up to Reva with his head bowed. She took them, tossed Crow his, then shouldered her own. "Well, don't just stand there. Go!"

Crow beamed at his wife. She was just as strong and decisive as he remembered. Anyone that dared confront her would learn their lesson the hard way—himself included.

When the gnome raced away, Crow slid closer to Reva.

"What do you think is out there?"

"Fuck if I know," she grumbled. "It's just one thing after another, isn't it?"

Crow sighed. It really was. "Living as long as we do, life would get pretty boring if fate didn't keep us on our toes."

Reva leveled a hard stare at him. "We've both had enough shit thrown our way to last ten fae lifetimes. Now, let's get out of here while the gnomes distract whatever is making that ruckus."

Crow took the map from his pocket and unfolded it, his eyes following the multiple routes they could take. The closest to the bottom of the mountain—the easiest for Reva to make a quick escape—was one of the first Crow had explored. The twisting lines of black ink faded over the years, and he prayed the gnomes hadn't carved any new pathways between here and there.

"This way," he said, leading them through blue-lit tunnels.

None of the gnomes stopped them. They were too busy racing to their own destinations, shouting about closing off entrances and getting the females and children in Gnome City to safety. Crow's conscience nagged at him at the mention of younglings.

"Do you think we should—"

"No," Reva said in a hurried voice.

He snapped his jaw shut and followed her around a narrow bend. "You didn't let me finish."

"We are *not* helping them, Crow."

The corner of his lips twitched into a smirk at how well she knew him, but fell back into a frown at the loud screeches from outside. "You're their queen now," he said, hesitating. Kings and queens were meant to protect their territory. That was what they were fighting for—a better world with rulers who cared.

Well, that, and revenge.

"Oh, please." She snorted. "I officially abdicate."

Crow swung his pack off his back and dug inside for a better weapon than the knife in his boot. Thankfully, the gnomes had stuffed his bracers inside, so he quickly fastened them in place. "I'm fairly certain that isn't how it works. You need to name a successor and make the statement official before—"

"The only reason we're fighting anything is if we have no other choice," she snapped.

Crow wrinkled his nose. It seemed to him there *was* no other choice unless they hid deep within the tunnels. And, in his opinion, being a coward was *never* an option. "Fine."

They came up to the exit, the light of the sun beckoning them forward. But the closer they got to escaping the tunnels, the clearer it became that the *worst* creatures had arrived in droves. Shadows flickered over the entrance in quick blips. One, then two, then a dozen. Then the sky blackened with their shadows.

"Do you want to wait for the gnomes to draw them away and make a break for it?" Crow asked. He hoped she said no— he didn't like leaving the gnomes on their own after Reva had just killed their ruler. They *had* been ready to serve him up to Reva like they'd undoubtedly done to hundreds of others, but it felt too much like genocide. Without their psychotic king and his orders, perhaps they would now change their ways.

Reva appeared to be seriously considering it for a moment before she gave a heavy sigh. "I can't fucking believe we're doing this," she hissed before charging forward with a faint crackle of green dancing along her fingers. Crow released the blades over his hands and followed.

They had only made it two steps outside when Reva stopped dead, her face paling. Crow pivoted, barely avoided slamming into her back, and followed her gaze. Thousands of large birds with brown and white speckled feathers soared overhead. Their massive talons were extended as if they had already selected their prey. Perhaps they had, as the mountainside was dotted with gnomes of every color. Arrows zipped toward them—the gnomes apparently trained in archery—but not many hit a target. The creatures were too fast, too agile.

Each of the agonized screeches shook Crow's bones and

made his ears ring. The birds jerked from side to side, avoiding arrows as well as colliding with each other. Some of them dove closer to the mountain and landed. Gnomes screamed as the birds' heavy bodies slammed into the rock—and other gnomes—with enough force to shake the mountain. Pebbles scattered from beneath their massive feet.

"What are they?" Crow whispered, blades at the ready, and hoped they wouldn't draw attention to themselves.

Reva heaved a few deep breaths. "That goblin-fucking piece of shit!"

Crow's eyes widened. He tugged his wife back into the shadows. "What?"

"They're sluaghs from where the West borders the North," Reva said through a clenched jaw. "Locasta took control of them while I was wicked."

Sluaghs—fae left homeless in the afterlife that wanted to make the living feel their pain—were exclusive to the West. Reva had always kept them contained as much as possible, but leave it to Locasta to weaponize them. This wasn't simply a physical attack either. It was a power-play to tell Reva that Locasta owned the West—whether because she'd discovered Langwidere was dead or because she refused to accept Thelia's authority.

Crow licked his lips. As vicious as the sluaghs were, they were Reva's subjects. "What do you want to do?"

"I'm going to send them home." She shoved away from Crow and stepped out into the light. Green crackled down her arms, making her hair sway in sync with the electricity, and she shot her magic straight into the sky without hitting a single fae.

The sluaghs' wings continued to beat in a long, slow motion, but they hovered in place, seemingly searching. Another blast of green light drew the eye of every bird. Reva waltzed farther out of the shadows, crackling, glowing, like the ruler she was.

"Go back to the West." The sluaghs seemed to hear her despite the low tone of her voice. "Go back and wait for me, your true ruler. Locasta no longer controls you."

A handful of words was all it took—something Locasta should've anticipated unless she assumed the Gnome King killed her already. The sluaghs very slowly, almost uncertainly, turned back the way they'd come, and the gnomes ceased defending their city. When the sky was clear, Reva kicked a large boulder. Green light blasted around her like a bubble. The magic tingled over Crow when it caught him in its radius, but didn't sting.

"My love?" he whispered.

The glow shrunk from a single large dome into two circles as she sucked the magic back into her hands. "Come on," Reva said between labored breaths. "We have a bitch to kill."

CHAPTER TWENTY-TWO

REVA

Reva watched the sluaghs disappear into the distance, the beat of their wings fading. She patted the Gnome King's stone in her pocket.

"We need to leave," Crow said.

They had maybe a quarter of a day's light left. Neither Crow nor Reva had gotten any sleep or anything to eat while at the palace, but they would just have to suck it up and carry on.

If they needed to, she was certain the gnomes would leave them alone if they stayed one more evening. But that was what Locasta would expect them to do. Hole themselves away… Just like they'd hid from her before Thelia was born. Or tried to, anyway.

The last time they'd hidden, Thelia was taken from them, and both Reva and Crow had been cursed. Once the sluaghs didn't report back to Locasta, the witch would find something else to send after them.

An idea struck Reva then. One that could possibly help the gnomes as well as them. She grabbed a dark brown gnome by the arm and spun him around. He appeared surprised but said nothing.

"Will you do something for me?" Reva asked, hunching down so they were of equal height.

He nodded. "Yes, my queen. Of course. What would you have me do?"

Reva placed her hands on both his shoulders, giving him her trust. "I told you if you followed my instructions, I would set you free. You won't be ruled by anyone anymore. Not a new Gnome King, me, or anyone else, understand? In order for Crow and I to save the Land of Oz, you can't mess this up."

"I will follow your orders." He clenched his staff. "To the ends of the world."

"You will not have to venture that far." Reva paused. "But your messenger will. I need a letter delivered to Locasta."

The gnome smiled. "You are a smart female. What would you like it to have?"

With a quick glance over her shoulder, she met Crow's eyes and could tell he already knew what she would say. She gripped the gnome's shoulders a bit firmer. "Don't tell Locasta that the Gnome King is dead. Send word that you killed me and in turn Crow escaped the palace. If you relay to her that Crow was murdered, she will retaliate against your kingdom. So make sure it's very clear he's still alive—just gone."

"I will do as you ask." He bowed his head. "Thank you, my queen, for your kindness. For allowing us to carry on."

Reva straightened, placing her arms back by her sides. "Good things will come your way—*if* you follow my instructions. Because I do believe in second chances. But only second chances, do you understand?"

"Yes, my queen. You're very generous." The gnome brushed past her and headed back inside the palace.

The sluaghs were now headed for their home at the Western border. Thelia would need Reva's training on how to handle them, but her daughter could do it. There was another reason that Reva had decided to give Thelia the West, rather than the East or the North, once she won them. The truth was she'd loved the West with every beat of her heart, but she'd destroyed it when she'd been cursed—hurt the fae she'd loved. So it had been for selfish reasons that she gave it to Thelia—because she was too frightened to return home, even though she wanted to see the faces of those she'd once known, who might still be alive. But she wanted a fresh start, and the West deserved someone in whom they could fully put their trust.

Crow brushed a hand through her hair, startling her out of her own thoughts.

"What's going on in there?" he asked, cradling the side of her head.

She grasped his hand and turned to face him, her gaze connecting with his. There was still so much unsaid between them and she wanted to give him this. "Thank you."

Crow arched a brow. "You know a fae is never supposed to say, 'thank you.'"

"Well, I just did." She shrugged. "Thank you. For always being the calm in my storm. Even after all this time."

He smiled, running his finger along her jaw. "Dearest Reva, did you actually give me a compliment?"

"Be quiet." She smirked. "Let's go before the sun sets. We should be able to get to Locasta's castle in less than two days. But we'll have to stop for the night, so I suggest we hurry."

"In that case, we run. We need to separate ourselves from the mountain as quickly as possible." Crow grabbed her hand then tugged her forward. She couldn't help but laugh as they sprinted out from the kingdom. It was no laughing matter, but this reminded her of old times, when she and Crow would chase each other and fall to the ground in a heap, then make love under the sun or the stars.

After running for a long while, they both came to a stop where bare trees were covered in light blue frost. Faeries in pale white gowns flew past her, creating snow flurries with their sheer wings. A cool breeze nipped at Reva's fingers, but her fae body was more resilient than a human's would be in this place.

They'd reached the North.

A crunching of twigs sounded close by and Crow yanked Reva from the path, behind a tree covered in ice. A few moments later a fae dressed in a Northern guard's uniform marched past them, sword swaying at his hip.

"I could have easily struck him down," Reva whispered.

"That would've only alerted Locasta when he didn't report back. And what if someone saw your magic?"

Crow was right. "Where should we stay the night?" she asked. "You know the North better than I do."

He smirked and tossed her his usual wink. "I know the perfect place, but you have to stay quiet until we get there. It won't be long."

Reva gave him a curious look. "Oh, so you have a secret place?"

"Mm-hmm." He held up a finger and smiled while waving her on. This had been his home, and while she'd heard most of his stories, uncovering new things about him was like meeting him for the first time.

With careful footsteps, she tried to avoid any sounds from the layer of frost, but that was impossible. Especially in a wooded area where wolves constantly darted by or ivory foxes would peek out from around trees and crawl up their trunks.

Eventually, as the sun lowered, a tiny village with a handful of cottages came into view. Each one was bright white like snow, with dark blue roofs twinkling with specks of silver. The wind picked up, and Reva shivered as she followed Crow to a home with a door that mirrored in color to its top. Icicles dangled from the arches, and Galanthus flowers were planted in a garden beside the porch, surrounded by patches of snow.

Smoke curled up from the chimney and lanterns shone through the lightly frosted window. Crow knocked softly on the painted wood. Almost immediately, footsteps sounded from inside. The door creaked open and a female poked her upper body out. Dark braids surrounded her head and brown eyes lit up when she gazed at Crow.

The female yanked open the door the remainder of the way and threw her arms around Crow, kissing his cheek. "You came home!"

"Home?" Reva asked, exchanging a look between the male and female. He'd told her he hadn't been with another female. Even before her, there had only ever been Locasta. "What *the fuck* is this?"

"Jealous already?" Crow inched back from the female and winked. "This is my sister, Calla."

"Sister? *Sister*?" Reva inhaled sharply. He'd never mentioned a sister, only that his parents had died from an avalanche when hiking in the mountains.

"Can we come inside, Calla?" Crow asked, already pulling Reva toward the door.

"Yes, yes." She let them both over the threshold and quickly closed the door behind them.

Crow chewed on his bottom lip. "I may have lied when I told you I had no family." He held up a finger. "But I told Calla never to tell anyone that she was related to me. If Locasta knew, she would use her against me."

Before Reva could say anything, two tiny fae children with curly black hair ran into the room grinning and chanting, "Crow. Crow." The two little females then stopped and ducked behind Calla's legs, peering around and looking at Reva. "Mama, who is that female?" one asked, the shape of her ears and cheekbones matching Calla's and Crow's.

Calla turned to her children, nudging them out from behind her. "Give him a hug and get back to bed."

With a quick swoop, Crow lifted them both, one in each arm. "Odette! Gemma! You've grown since I was here last. How old are you now? Fifteen? *Twenty?*" He gave each giggling child a kiss on the cheek before setting them down. They dashed back into their room with one last curious look at Reva.

Calla turned back around and placed her hands on her hips. "I'm curious who you are as well." Her smile was warm, one of the warmest Reva had ever seen. Reva tried to return the expression, but the grimace felt frozen on her face.

"This is my wife," Crow said softly so that only Calla and Reva could hear.

Calla's eyes widened and she covered her mouth. "Are you an idiot, Crow? When? The last time you came was a year ago and you mentioned no one."

"It's a long, long story, Calla."

"We have time. Sit." She pointed Crow and Reva to the settee as though they were children. Reva took a seat and fought back a smile at how Calla bossed her brother around. Along the floor in front of the fire was a rug made of wolf fur. Paintings of wintry trees and animals hung all over the room that she assumed were created by Odette and Gemma since they were each signed with an O or G.

Calla remained standing and continued, "You come back to the North, where you know *she* lives, and you bring a wife? Are you trying to bait Locasta into a fight?"

"Not just a wife," Crow said. "I never told you everything. This is *Reva*. I married Reva of the West over twenty years ago."

Calla's lips parted and her hand flew up to cover her mouth. "The Wicked Witch!" she exclaimed. "What did you do? She was dead!"

Crow stood and lightly grabbed his sister by the wrists. "Listen, she was cursed, like me. Only different. And she was never really dead."

"She nearly brought Oz to ruination!" Calla whisper-shouted.

In that moment, Reva lost all her confidence. This was the reaction she'd feared from anyone who'd heard about her return. She'd been lucky that Falyn had been sympathetic toward her when she'd met her at the brothel. But that was apparently the rare exception to the rule.

"Locasta found us the night Reva bore our daughter, Thelia. She hid our child away in the human world, and cursed us both."

"A child?" Calla nearly screeched. "Where is she now? You went for her after your curse was broken, I assume."

Crow smiled. "She's the one who broke it. Dorothy is Thelia."

"What in the ever-loving Oz..." Calla pressed her fingers to her temples. "I think I need to make us all a drink."

"Where's Jovie?" Crow asked.

"My husband's on guard duty for the next few weeks, patrolling the palace. Things are getting worse here. It had been the safest territory, but now it's becoming like everywhere else. Locasta is finally starting to show her true colors, the ones you've spoken of for all these years."

"So we've heard," Reva said, thinking about Birch and how his parents were dead because of Locasta. "I know this won't make you think differently of me, but we're going to try and make Oz better again. I vow it."

"If you were cursed like my brother was, it wasn't your fault." Calla turned around and headed into the kitchen.

"She hates me," Reva whispered.

"No." Crow chuckled. "She's making you a drink. That means she likes you."

Calla came back into the room with a bottle of rum and two glasses. For a moment, Reva wondered if Calla would attempt to poison her for all she'd done in her past, but she quickly brushed that off.

Crow's sister poured each of them a drink, then sipped from the bottle as she settled herself into one of the chairs.

"We're only staying for the night," Crow said after taking a swig from his glass. "But I promise, the next time we meet, I'll stay longer."

"You two can stay in my room and I'll sleep on the settee."

"No, no," Reva interrupted. "We'll sleep in here. And I won't hear another word of it." She was finally feeling a bit back to herself after downing her drink and letting it warm her a bit.

"If that's what you wish to do. I can't deny a ruler." Calla smiled.

For a while longer, they filled Calla in on their travels so far, while Crow's sister spoke of her husband and children. Then Calla left them alone in the sitting room while she turned in for the night. Reva hoped if everyone could see she'd been cursed by Locasta, they would accept her back. There was a nagging worry they wouldn't, but there was also the relief that Crow's sister had seemed to like her.

The evening was surprisingly quiet, but that must have been because the night beasts were busy terrorizing the Emerald City or other territories. Locasta had her guards to do that for her in the North.

Crow lowered himself on the rug in front of the crackling fire. He held an arm open and beckoned Reva next to him.

She got up and removed her boots before tucking herself beside him and placing her head on his chest. "Your sister's nice. I can see why you want to protect her, and I'm glad you allowed me to meet her." Reva's own sister was gone, Ozma was hopefully still all right, and Whispa either remained a night beast or dead. She couldn't allow herself to dwell on what she couldn't help, no matter how much it hurt.

"Of course, she's nice. She takes after me."

"You know how to ruin a moment," she teased, holding him tighter.

The Gnome King's stone felt heavy in her pocket and she drew it out. She held it up so the flames flickered against its red surface. "How do you think it came to be inside him?"

Crow exhaled. "I should have figured it out before. Ceres and his wife weren't always stone. They'd been flesh and bone once, though I could never find a reason for the change. It makes sense..."

"What does?" Reva fisted the stone protectively.

"When Ceres and his queen became stone, their hearts must've hardened too. Like Tin's, only more so."

"So if their hearts became such powerful stones—"

"That means someone has the former queen's heart," Crow finished. "And how the story must have been told. Although, a very vague story indeed since it failed to mention the stone was inside the asshole."

Reva released a low chuckle and held him tighter after tucking the stone away.

He drew light circles on her arm. "If we weren't at my sister's with little ones here, I would worship your body for the remainder of the night."

In a quick motion, Reva was on top of him, her nose brushing his. "There are different ways to worship a body."

Without further words, his mouth caught hers and he caressed her lips as if they'd just met, deepening and deepening the kiss. Despite the fact that they were married with a grown child together, this somehow felt like their first kiss all over again. She never wanted to forget this moment, or any with him, whether good or bad, and she couldn't help but remember their first kiss.

"You don't know what you're talking about," Reva spat. Trying to tell everyone that Locasta wasn't good would be harder than they'd thought.

"Oh, I don't?" Crow frowned.

Reva took the map of the North from Crow's hand. He stumbled back, taking her with him, and knocking them both to the floor.

"You're an idiot," she said, but couldn't control herself from laughing. She'd never laughed as much as she did around this male who had stumbled upon her weeks ago, requesting help from her.

"I rather enjoy your laugh." He laced his hands through her hair and neither moved. Not until he lifted his head and brought her face to his, then kissed her softly.

Reva pulled back, only a minimal distance. "I told you I wouldn't kiss you first." Then she pressed her mouth back to his.

There were kisses then and there were kisses now. Reva had

told him that he was the calm to her storm. But right then, it felt like the calm before the storm that would end Locasta.

CHAPTER TWENTY-THREE

CROW

Bidding Calla goodbye was always difficult, but this time was worse. If Crow and Reva failed to defeat Locasta, this could be the final farewell he had always feared. Calla would be fine—he had to believe that. Their relationship was kept a secret for her sake, but Locasta's fury could affect the entire North. He'd finished the breakfast of warm oats his sister had made—repeating in his mind that her family would be safe—and now lounged on the floor with her daughters, playing a counting game with stones. The last time he'd visited, both Gemma and Odette had only wanted to build with their blocks. Hopefully they would play again one day.

"Are you sure this is wise?" Calla asked him quietly.

Crow darted a quick glance at Reva. She sat beside the fire, staring, unblinking, into the flames. "I'm rarely sure that anything I do is wise," he joked, winking at the children so they knew he wasn't serious.

Calla pursed her lips and tapped the younglings on their shoulders. "Go play outside for a minute, please." Their bottom lips stuck out in exaggerated pouts but they scurried off without voicing their annoyance, leaving their rocks behind. "You can't seriously think you should walk into the palace as if it were nothing."

Crow sighed. He and Reva had told his sister their plan before the children woke, and she was far from happy. But too many things in his life had been kept from Calla, Reva included. He had always wanted to speak with her about his beloved wife but worried about her reaction to *who* he'd promised his life to. Given all the horrible things Reva had done as the Wicked Witch, it was an honest concern. And if he had told Calla about Thelia, it would have raised the question of his child's mother. When Thelia was in the mortal world, there had been no chance of Calla meeting her, so he'd chosen not to burden his sister with the information. Now that he was marching to possible death, Crow wanted her to know what they were doing, and why, in case things went poorly.

"What would you suggest we do instead?" he asked.

"Not strut back through that bitch's front door as a distraction," she hissed. "There's bound to be another way for you and Reva to sneak inside."

Crow took her hand and squeezed reassuringly. "I'll come back, Calla. And when I do, the North will be free. *You*, my sister, will be free."

"Don't make promises you can't keep, Crow." She gave him a lingering look, her eyes glistening with unshed tears. "I hate that you keep putting yourself in this position. It isn't your job to save Oz."

He smiled a small, sad smile. She wasn't wrong—it wasn't his job—but someone had to step up. If not him, then who? "Oz is in this state because good fae did nothing."

Reva stood, the movement catching his eye. "We should leave before there are too many witnesses on the brick road to the palace."

Crow nodded, climbed to his feet, and embraced his sister.

"Keep the rum out. We may need it on the way back through."

Calla sniffled into his shoulder. The last time she'd cried over his leaving was right after their parents died. It felt like ten lifetimes ago that he'd entered Locasta's palace to work as an official messenger—a task well-suited to his bird form. He'd had to support his sister back then, even if it meant living apart and sending coin home. If anyone discovered he had a family member solely dependent on him, he never would've gotten the job as a guard. For a moment, he held tighter. How different would things have turned out if he had gotten another job—*any* other job? Though, he couldn't wish away that part of his past. If not for Locasta, he never would've gone looking for Reva's help, and Thelia wouldn't exist.

"You be safe." Calla pulled away from Crow and turned to Reva, pulling her close. "And you too."

Although she appeared slightly uncomfortable with the hug, Reva wrapped her arms around his sister.

Crow and Reva stepped out into the crisp, cold winter air, sparing another moment for him to give Odette and Gemma a quick hug. They seemed to have warmed slightly to Reva's presence—though she received no embrace, they offered her smiles and waves. His heart grew heavier the more space he put between them and his sister's home. For all his brave words, Crow knew that Locasta wouldn't hesitate to reclaim him. But first there would be torture if Reva took too long with her part of the plan.

"You're clear on where to go?" he asked for what felt like the hundredth time. "Where to steal the servant uniform and how to get into the kitchens?"

"Yes," she said patiently. Then, as if understanding why he asked, she added, "It will all go according to plan."

It needed to. One slip up, one miscalculation, and, if the stone didn't work, they would both be cursed again. Or worse. It had all seemed like a much better idea when they'd discussed it the night before. What if Locasta only cursed him and killed

Reva? He had already gone through that agony once. If it weren't for the other drastic changes last time, like his curse being broken and realizing who Thelia was, he surely would've followed Reva to the grave with a broken heart.

When the top of Locasta's palace came into view, Crow tugged Reva off the yellow brick road. This was to be where they parted ways temporarily, but panic clawed at his insides. "Maybe we should find more help before we do this." His voice cracked slightly. "Tin would come."

"He needs to stay with Thelia," Reva reminded him. "And he's been through enough as it is. We all have."

Right. He knew that. It was more important that their daughter had Tin's protection since she couldn't control her magic at will yet. But the sight of his old home—his prison—left his mind spinning. For years he'd lived inside those pearly white walls, warmed himself by the fireplaces, nourished himself with fruit from the private orchards. But he'd also suffered. Locasta's temper was quick to rise and slow to fade. After years of trying to leave, he'd finally succeeded to break through her magic holding him there.

"I'll be right behind you." Reva cupped his cheeks with her palms. "Take the stone."

An image of her face covered with green pustules rose in his mind, and he shoved the memory away. "I told you this morning, no. And I meant it." Crow swallowed hard, then pressed a desperate, hard kiss to her lips. "Don't get caught."

"Who is underestimating who this time?" She gently pushed at his chest and lowered his mask from the top of his head to cover his face. "Let's get moving. The sooner we kill Locasta, the sooner we can truly start our lives together."

"I love you," he whispered, and forced himself to walk away.

Each step he took revealed another inch of the palace. The roof. Decorative, snow-capped trees. Curling parapets. Arched windows. Long balconies. Red winter-blooming flowers. Then, finally, the massive frost-covered doors. The guards weren't visible—Locasta wanted to appear confident in her safety—but they were there. Watching. Always watching. He felt the weight of their eyes on him as he neared a snowy drawbridge and paused. It was the last thing between him and Locasta's lair. Well, the bridge and, undoubtedly, dozens of guards.

It took everything in Crow not to extend his blades as he took that first step forward. He sensed the guards closing in on him when he reached the doors. Should he knock? It wasn't like they weren't expecting him at this point—they would have seen him walking brazenly up to the palace. He took a shuddering breath—possibly the last he would take as a free male—and shoved the doors inward. His stomach churned as he lifted his chin and waltzed into the palace.

The glittering entry was exactly how he'd remembered it. White marble floors so clean they looked like mirrors, columns of granite wrapped in sheer, flowing silver fabric, and a large table with an arrangement of winter flowers. A chandelier made of bone-white antlers hung from the high ceiling.

Guards were waiting, as he knew they would be, but only six. They were elves—Locasta's personal preference for those working within her palace—and wore pine-colored uniforms that hugged their lithe bodies. Rust-colored buttons ran down their chests in two rows and, inside, their jackets were lined with fur. The serrated swords they held were less worrisome to Crow than the palace itself.

"Good morning," Crow said as cheerfully as possible. If they could've heard his erratic pulse, they would've known how much of a lie his nonchalant tone was. "I believe Locasta has been looking for me."

The shortest guard eyed the feathers in Crow's hair and recognition slowly filtered in. He grunted in distaste. "She's waiting for you in the banquet hall."

Crow took a step forward and all six of the guards stiffened. "The hall is that way," he said with a casual wave of his hand. "I know the way, if you'll simply clear a path."

"You know we can't let you wander the palace alone," said a female.

Of course, they couldn't—he was a threat. But only warranted six armed escorts, apparently. That wasn't enough to clear the way for Reva. He needed every available guard looking at him so his wife could come in unnoticed. "Then, by all means…" Crow walked slowly toward them this time, hands raised to show he carried no weapon.

They stood rigidly at his approach but didn't move to stop him. Once he was in the middle of the guards—two in front, two behind, and one on each side—he let his hands fall to his sides. He held his breath for a moment before extending the blades from his bracers and spun with lightning speed, slicing four guards down where they stood. Blood sprayed against the pristine walls. The fifth, he pulled to his chest and placed the blades carefully against the artery in her neck. Warm liquid flowed over his fingers as he pressed the blades into her skin as a warning.

"Now, now," Crow told the last guard. The female froze mid-attack. "I mean you no harm."

He truly didn't, but some things were unavoidable. Four dead fae would undoubtedly bring the rest of the palace guards rushing to investigate, leaving Reva's path clear.

Boots slapped against the floors. Dozens upon dozens of guards. Crow smiled to himself. "It isn't polite to keep a lady waiting," he said, tossing the guard at her comrade, and raced down the glistening hall.

He ran past tapestries of gold and gilded mirrors. Deep blue curtains pleated around window frames. The rust-colored stains where Locasta had broken his bird form years ago still colored the tile at the bottom of a grand staircase. The guards closed in on him just as he caught a glimpse of a tarnished cage hanging in front of the highest window in the palace. One of *his* many cages. One of the many that Locasta had kept him in as a bird when he'd angered her. Another was bolted to the wall across the room.

"Stop," a male shouted.

Crow tore his eyes from the cage and then—finally—shouldered his way into the banquet hall. He slammed the doors shut behind him and flicked the lock. An enormous table stretched the length of the room with trays of food stacked high from one end to the other. Burgundy and bronze décor dripped down the walls and candles hung from the ceiling, their warm glow filling the room. The hardwood floors were stained ebony with a thick crème-colored rug covering the center.

But the splendor of the room failed to hold his attention when the female who had destroyed Crow's life stared at him from a high-backed chair.

Locasta's obsidian hair flowed over her shoulders and her fair skin practically glowed in the candlelight. She wore a dress of ice blue with silver gems sewn into the bodice. "Crow." Her light, airy voice made his skin crawl. It was an innocent voice, a deceptive one. She steepled her fingers, elbows on the lace tablecloth, and lifted her ruby lips into a savage smile. "I'd like to say this is unexpected, but, well…"

Guards slammed into the doors and the hinges rattled. Crow fought to keep his body from shaking. Locasta looked Crow up and down before standing and rounding the table. He wanted so badly to move away, but Reva would be there soon. He could endure long enough for her to avoid detection. "Is this my welcome party then?"

"Oh, my darling, if only it were. I've spent years thinking of new ways to break you after your last visit, but first…" Locasta knocked Crow's mask to the floor and slapped him across the cheek, the blood rushing to his face at the sting. She lifted a lock of his hair and ran it between her fingers. "I heard a rumor that a certain acquaintance of ours managed to resurrect herself, only to meet her end a second time."

Crow kept his breaths steady, hiding a smile. The gnomes had listened to Reva and passed on the news of her *death*. No one in the palace would be expecting her. "Don't speak to me about Reva."

"Is it revenge you really want? Because I don't think it is." She twisted the lock of his hair around her hand until his scalp throbbed. "I think you're secretly pleased. Now we can truly move on together. After your punishment, that is."

Locasta stepped closer. He felt her breath on his ear, then wet warmth as she licked the lobe. "Tell me, my lovely bird, do you want the chains or the ropes before we fuck?"

Crow leaned away from her, snapped his hand around her neck, and gave a firm squeeze in one fluid movement. "I could kill you now."

Locasta laughed, moving her hand from his hair to caress his red cheek. "How many nights did you lay awake, naked in my bed, and *wish* you could squeeze the air from my lungs? And how many times did you even try?"

Shame blazed through him. Countless times he had wanted to kill her, yet he had never tried. Not even once. But he would do it now. After everything Locasta had done to him, to Reva, and Thelia, he would kill her with a smile on his face.

But he kept his promises, especially those he made to Reva. His wife would be the one to deal the final blow to the Northern Witch.

"Precisely," Locasta cooed as if knowing he wasn't going to kill her. "Now is no different."

A shadow slipped along the wall behind Locasta. Crow released her throat, clutching her wrist instead. Squeezing and squeezing until he was sure the bones would snap.

"No," Crow started as a faint green light flickered to life. "Now *everything* is different."

Chapter Twenty-Four

Reva

Another terrible experience to add to this journey—hiding in the shadows before knocking out a defenseless servant and stealing her uniform. It was too loose, the fabric itched her skin like Glinda's clothing had, and she already missed the black. The white hue reminded her of Langwidere's obsession with that color, only this was nowhere near seductive.

As she slipped through the back entrance of the palace, into the kitchens to which Crow had given her directions, she spotted a single female with her hair in two braided buns. She kneaded dough along a silver counter in front of a blue and white striped wall. "Laundry's over there," the female said as she shaped the bread, then glanced up. "Another new face—I'm not surprised. Hopefully you last longer than the others."

Reva spotted a bowl full of fruit on the edge of a table and pressed an apple into the pocket of her apron. She would need something sweet to bite into when this was all over. *If* it ended well.

"I'm sure I will." Reva picked up the large wicker basket

filled with soiled clothing and towels. The smell of peppermint permeated the air as she walked through the kitchen and entered a pale blue hallway covered in black feathers. The feathers were attached to the walls in artful, swirled patterns. Her stomach sank at the sight of them. These weren't just any bird's feathers—she recognized them right away. *Crow's*.

Reva had heard the stories from her husband. Locasta wouldn't only use the feathers for her *art* that he'd shed—she would pluck them from Crow's bird form when she was livid with him. But Reva hadn't known that Locasta was obsessed enough to hang them as decorations in her hallways. This would not go on any longer—no matter if she had to rip the Northern Witch to shreds with her own teeth and hands.

The stone rested in her apron pocket beside the apple, and she stroked her fingers against its cool surface to reassure herself that it was indeed still there. Crow had refused to take it, even when she'd tried to sneak it into his pocket.

After leaving the basket of laundry behind, she turned down another long hallway with a neat line of paintings on each side of the walls—all of Locasta in seductive poses—naked. Before Reva lost her stomach, two familiar voices echoed from behind the servants' entrance to the banquet room. Crow and *the bitch*.

Tiptoeing as quietly as she could, she pushed open the door and peered in, her gaze landing on the duo. Crow's hand was latched around Locasta's throat and all the bitch did was smile at him, seeming to not believe he would end her life. Reva focused on Locasta's hand. The witch's fingers twitched, and Reva knew she was about to do something tricky.

The magic thrummed through Reva, lightning crackling as she slipped through the door and stepped into the room.

Crow said something to Locasta as he released her throat and grabbed her wrist.

The Northern Witch looked up at Reva, her lips parting and brows lifting in surprise. "You're supposed to be dead." Locasta's fingers twitched again and worry spread across Crow's face.

Reva shook her head. "I wouldn't try that, Locasta."

"I should have known those gnome bastards were traitors." She elbowed Crow in the ribs, causing him to gasp and free her. "You're going to the bird cage now. Then perhaps to the cornfield until you crawl back to me with broken bones."

"Stab her!" Reva shrieked.

Crow didn't hesitate to release his blades and thrust them into Locasta's stomach with a squelch, spilling crimson down her blue gown.

Shimmering, pale-blue light flickered around Locasta as she thrust a hand out. Crow's skin changed to the same color as Locasta's magic, and he transformed into his bird form before vanishing.

Reva started to cry out when a *caw* came from a cage bolted to the far side of the room. Reva flung a burst of magic at the Northern Witch. Despite gripping her wounded stomach, Locasta still managed to turn the green lightning into bright white snowflakes.

"Ah, this brings back such wonderful memories," Locasta rasped, a thin line of blood trickling from the edge of her mouth. "Are you so desperate to become my plaything again?"

A flash of blue magic barreled toward Reva. She dodged to the left, but a hard hit struck her arm, turning into a sharp ache. It spread and spread, growing hotter until she couldn't bear it. A scream broke free from Reva, and she glanced down at her skin as Locasta laughed again. Green rippled up Reva's flesh and pustules bubbled.

Why isn't the stone working? It was supposed to prevent Locasta's shifting magic. In that moment Reva couldn't help but worry for Thelia. What would Locasta do to her daughter this time?

With a shaking hand, Reva reached into the front pocket of her apron. As soon as her fingers brushed the stone, a warm energy spread through her, taking away the scalding sensation.

Her skin was no longer green and bubbling, but smooth and pale.

"What have you got there?" Locasta asked after Reva tugged out the Gnome King's glimmering heart.

Reva focused on Locasta, who was growing paler with each passing moment. She wasn't willing to let the witch lose consciousness and die in peace. Not after everything she'd done.

"It's a gift from the Gnome King." Reva smiled, baring her teeth. "After I reduced him to rubble."

Locasta hurled another ball of magic at Reva. It hit her in the chest, but this time she didn't even feel it.

"You'll never take him from me again!" Locasta shouted, blowing the doors wide open with her magic. "Guards!"

As the guards burst into the room, Reva let her energy spill out, lightning crackling all around her. "Do you really want to mess with me? I am Reva and was once the Wicked Witch of the West because of your ruler. Everything that has happened is because of her."

The guards didn't move—only stared in horror at Reva, likely knowing they would be helpless against her magic.

"Seems like they will easily choose my side over yours, bitch," Reva spat at Locasta. She launched another bolt of lightning at Locasta, which again turned into bright white flurries, falling to the floor.

She clenched the stone tighter, and a heavy quake erupted beneath their feet. The rumbling sounds reverberated within the room, rattling the frames hanging on the pearly white walls. Green lightning wove around Reva, like snakes crossing over one another. She smiled with menace and walked toward Crow's cage to open it. Locasta hadn't moved a muscle toward them, yet she watched with fury blazing in her eyes. Crow flew out, flapping his wings fiercely. She opened a small space in her magic, allowing Crow to pass through and perch himself on her shoulder.

"You're right." Reva grinned wider. "Crow will watch. But it will be as I repay you for all you've done to him, my daughter, and *me*."

"Ah, yes." Locasta coughed, specks of blood spotting her chin, her eyes filled with rage. "Your *daughter*. However, I did raise the true Dorothy Gale for a long time, toyed with her until she wasn't worth my time anymore, then handed her off to Langwidere. The game isn't over yet." She glanced toward the top of the stairs and screamed, "Kill her!"

Reva glanced upward as a storm of wings rose and drew closer. The night beasts.

Howls carried through the room as cursed pixies shot out, one after another, and Reva thought it would never end.

Above her and Crow, the cursed pixies' skeletal forms swirled in a circle, waiting for the right opportunity to attack. One with a twisted spine and a row full of sharp teeth took the chance, and struck Reva's magic, which sliced the pixie in half. Another flew in at the same time, scratching Reva across the cheek with its deadly claws, just before her magic darkened it to ash.

The night beasts continued to hover—but something was awry. Same as in the forest when she'd run from them with Crow, more of the pixies appeared hesitant to attack than not. And she didn't think it was because of her magic.

"Kill her now!" Locasta seethed, falling to her knees. "Or tonight, I shall rip your wings from your bodies and feed them to Crow."

"Without your power to use against me, you are *nothing*," Reva said in a low, but deadly, voice. "Even after your curse when I was without my magic, I was something. I've been through worse things than you, and you've mistreated our land long enough."

"What a sad, sad speech that was." Locasta cocked her head, chest heaving. "But just remember, I fucked Crow first."

Crow's talons dug into Reva's shoulder and her blood boiled at the taunt, more so for her husband than herself. He'd been through enough of this shit already. She flicked her gaze at the cursed pixies once more and shouted, "If you want this to be over, then end her."

Locasta cackled. "You're a fool! They won't listen to you."

A few moments passed, and Reva started to believe Locasta was right. But then one pixie, with uneven leathery wings, finally parted from the pack and barreled toward the Northern Witch. Another broke from the group, then another. More continued to follow. Reva reeled her magic in enough to give the cursed pixies room as they shrieked and tore through Locasta. But not all. A few tried to get to Reva and Crow, failing as their bodies flopped to the floor with a sickening plop.

Howls of agony escaped Locasta's lips as the pixies ripped into her flesh. Blood speckled the walls, and pooled along the marble floor as skin, muscle, and organs were torn away from her bones. Reva had wanted to kill Locasta herself, but having Crow stab her and the pixies finish her off was the right choice. The cursed pixies had been slaves to Locasta even longer than she'd been.

As the cursed pixies broke away from the body and roared with glee, there was nothing but Locasta's skeleton left behind, her jaw open as though still screaming, even in death. *Good.*

Low wails came from the cursed pixies as they dropped to the floor with thump after thump, trembling until their bodies stilled. Were they dead? Reva reeled her power back in, lightning no longer crackling. Crow flew from her shoulder and transformed in a cloud of smoke, a few black feathers cascading downward.

Reva tucked the stone into her apron and hurried to a small skeletal pixie. Its eyes were still open, its chest moving. The dark color of its body slowly started to fade to a light brown. Its spine straightened, teeth no longer fangs, wings thinning, skin thickening. The curse was broken, and the beast returned to his pixie form—with pointy ears, light hair, and a handsome face.

"Reva? Crow?" a female pixie whispered from behind her. Reva's eyes widened and she whipped her head around. This one wore a tattered red and blue dress that fell to her ankles. Her gray hair was mussed and her honey-colored eyes exhausted, but there was a smile on her face.

"Whispa!" Reva shouted, her heart racing with excitement. "You're alive."

"I don't think I want to do that again." Whispa pushed herself to her feet and brushed her matted hair out of her eyes. "And I don't think you do either."

Tears streaked Reva's cheeks and she swiped them away as she stood. She rushed toward her old friend and folded her arms around the pixie, squeezing her tight.

Circling her, all the pixies—now uncursed—were silent, watching them. And so was Crow. Whispa removed herself from Reva and gave Crow a similar hug. "I'm sorry I couldn't have prevented this, but I was the first to go after her this time."

"That was you who broke from the pack first?" Reva asked. "You did good, Whispa. As for the last time, no one could have stopped Locasta that fateful night." They'd tried to hide and had done the best they could at the time. She turned toward the others, who seemed to be waiting for her command. "You're free. Go home."

Some nodded and left the room, but most didn't. They stayed, surprising her. A female with bright red curls and a heart-shaped face shifted forward. "What do you want us to do next?"

Reva smiled at the determination in the way they stood with their spines straightened and chins lifted. "How about we start by cleaning up the North, then working on the East?" She looked back at Whispa. "Can you send word to our new leader—Thelia—of the South and the West to meet us at the protected tavern in the Emerald City in two weeks' time? I have a good feeling the capital will be safe by then. Thelia is located in Glinda's palace."

"Of course." Whispa bowed. "For you, my friend, I will always help."

Taking a step back, Reva turned around to find Crow looking

at the walls, the marble floor, and his *cage*. Reva wondered for a moment if she'd been selfish. She'd told herself she would take Locasta's palace and make it her own, but did Crow even want it to be his? After all he'd gone through here?

She would choose to go wherever he wished. "We can leave if you want, Crow. We can build our own palace somewhere else in the North or stay in the East."

"No," Crow said firmly. "The palace never made me feel unsafe. It was *her*. Always her. The North was home to me, but so was the West. I say we make this ours, not hide from her shadow. We can easily paint everything black." He winked at her. And with that wink, she knew he would eventually be all right.

"You know me so well." Reva bit her lip and pushed her hand into her apron pocket, fishing out the apple. "My gift to you." She handed him the fruit.

"Oh, you must really love me." He grinned, taking the apple and biting into it.

"Once you finish that, we need to get this bitch out of here." She pointed at Locasta's remains, believing the witch still merited worse, but this would have to do.

"First, take a bite. You deserve it."

Reva opened her mouth and Crow pressed the apple between her teeth. It tasted like victory.

CHAPTER TWENTY-FIVE

CROW

The room slowly cleared of pixies. Reva had appeared much more collected than he'd felt in those first few minutes after Locasta's death—giving jobs to those who remained—while his mind was a whirlwind of thoughts.

They'd won.

Whispa was back.

The North and East were free.

His sister's family was safe.

And yet, there was still so much more work to do to return Oz to its former glory. That was for another day, though. It was all he could do not to collapse with relief. Locasta was *dead*. She'd gotten exactly what she deserved when Reva sent the pixies after her. He hoped that they felt half as good about ripping into Locasta as he had felt stabbing her. The blades hadn't inflicted nearly enough pain to make up for everything she'd done to him over the years, but it was better than nothing. Vengeance had needed to be shared among those she'd wronged, and that was a long list. Thelia deserved to share in it too, but she was doing far greater things than seeking revenge against a female she'd never known.

"Are you all right?" Reva asked again when the door clanged shut behind the final pixie.

A red stain was all that remained of Locasta now—her bones carried away by grateful palace guards. Crow wondered briefly what they would do with them, but couldn't find it in himself to care. "Yes. I'm fine," he assured her, tossing his apple core onto the table. He was more than all right—just shocked. "Though, I almost think I'm dreaming."

Reva leaned up and kissed him on the cheek. "You're wide awake."

Crow's lips quirked into a smile. "If we're staying here for the night, I want to show you something."

Reva's brows rose. "Now?"

"You can order the guards around some more on the way," he joked.

She took his hand with a huff. "I think I've given them enough tasks for the moment."

"The next moment?" Crow laughed as he led her from the banquet hall. "They'll be busy for days, and I *know* you're not done yet."

"You know me too well."

Crow kept his eyes on the marble floor, not wanting to see the familiar décor again. Once Reva changed things, he would feel comfortable in the halls, but not truly until then. Especially not when his feathers hung like tapestries, and cages loomed in almost every room. The guards seemed hard at work on removing them, as per Reva's first order as Witch of the North, which was a relief.

"Not even Locasta knew about this place," Crow whispered when they turned the final corner toward their destination. "I found it completely by accident."

Reva's eyes gleamed with interest. "Oh? What kind of accident?"

Over the years, before their curses, Crow had shared many stories of his time with Locasta, but he wasn't sure he wanted to tell Reva this particular one. He'd been in his cage for days when Locasta finally decided to free him, and she only did that because she was leaving the palace and didn't want him to starve. Anger drove him to destroy multiple paintings in the hallways while she was away, tearing them from their frames and lighting them on fire. When he'd come upon a hideous, dust-covered statue, he'd intended to push it over. Break it apart. Destroy it completely. But it hadn't budged, which had only angered him more. He'd found the switch because his next attempt was to pry it apart piece by piece. The tale didn't paint him in the best light, but it ended well.

"A happy one." Crow winked and stopped in front of the statue. Pieces of smooth driftwood were held together with copper spikes forming a five-foot egg shape. He'd always hated the statue, up until he'd found the secret it contained.

"Prepare to be amazed," he told Reva, and released her hand so he could kneel to reach the hidden lever.

A moment later, a panel of the wall lifted smoothly into the ceiling, revealing a rather large room. Floating yellow lights flickered to life as they stepped inside. The walls were unpolished dark stone and the floor was covered in a plush brown throw rug. Stacks of dust-covered books lined the walls. In the very center of the room sat a round bed covered in gold silk. How many hours had he spent curled up there? Countless. Whenever Locasta was away or when she was preoccupied, he would slip inside and read until his eyes grew heavy. If it was the latter, it was too dangerous to fall asleep there and risk Locasta noticing his absence, but the precious moments of freedom spent within these secret walls had kept Crow going.

"It feels like you in here," Reva said.

He knocked a cobweb down from the ceiling and grinned. "Old and dirty?" Reva's eyes widened as he slid an arm around her waist. "Shall we see which is dirtier?"

"Crow." She batted playfully at him. "There's so much to do before we—"

He swooped in and kissed her fiercely. There would be plenty of time to set things in motion, but standing there, in his space, knowing they were done for a moment... He *needed* her now. He deepened the kiss, his fingers tangling in her hair.

Reva melted into him. Her lips were hot on his, moving as urgently as his own, and he knew she needed this too. When his tongue skated along her bottom lip, she moaned into him before greeting it with her own, causing Crow's hard cock to press painfully against his pants.

His breath hitched when she slipped her hands beneath his shirt, searing his skin. And that was it. He couldn't stand waiting any longer. One moment they stood in the entrance of his sanctuary, the next Reva was pressed against the wall.

"Clothes," he growled against her mouth. He needed her *now*. "Off."

Reva shoved him back a step and their heavy breaths filled the room. Fabric tore loudly. Crow couldn't tell which article of clothing had ripped or who it belonged to because they were both moving as frantically as the other to rid themselves of the unwanted barriers. Neither of them bothered with their shirts.

The second Reva stood after pulling her pants from her feet, Crow lifted her. Her legs automatically wrapped around his waist, holding him tightly. The tip of his cock rubbed against her wetness, teasing him. Her tongue then ran up the side of his neck and he nearly lost control.

Using the wall to brace them both, Crow slipped inside her. His moan echoed through the dusty room. Reva threw her head back, her nails digging into his shoulders. A string of mumbled words fell from her mouth.

Crow pulled back until he was nearly out of her, then slid slowly inside again. He ground his teeth, forcing himself not to lose control. At least, not until Reva was satisfied.

"Crow," Reva whispered in his ear. One hand left his

shoulders to scrape down his back. "Stop playing around and fuck me!"

A small grin found its way to his lips. "If you insist."

Crow moved faster. Slammed harder. The floating lights seemed to shimmer brighter with each thrust, until he buried his face in Reva's neck, and pressed his eyes shut. Just a little longer before he could let go... He wasn't sure he could make it...

Reva cried out in pleasure and he released the harsh breath he was holding. Then he released something else, a stream of vibrations soaring through him as he shouted her name. They both froze, panting. His heart felt as if it would break through his chest. It had been a long time since he'd experienced such a desperate need—or the pure exhaustion that followed. His legs quaked beneath him and, if it weren't for the wall behind Reva, he might've dropped them both to the floor.

"I love you," he breathed. The scent of Reva mixed with sweat and dust and pleasure. "So much."

"I love you too," she said, wrapping her arms around his neck to help support her weight. "Can you put me down now?"

"Do I have to?" he teased as he set Reva back on her feet. He brushed the hair out of her face. There were no words that could express how he felt about his wife, and the gravity of their love slammed into him like a bolt of lightning. If he had things his way, he would never let Reva out of his sight again, but that wasn't realistic. Nor would she allow it, which was another reason he loved her. His strong, independent, beautiful, powerful—

"What's that look for?" she asked. "It looks like you're plotting something that will get us both in trouble."

Crow shook himself back to reality. "What look?"

"Never mind," Reva said with a roll of her eyes.

"So...?" he asked with a crooked grin.

Reva wobbled slightly before stepping into her pants and shot him a quizzical look. "What?"

"Which is dirtier? Me, or the room?"

She rolled her eyes. "I know which one is *older*."

He leaned in and kissed her cheek. "You're older than I am."

"Crow!" Reva swatted at him. "Get dressed. We have plans to make."

Chuckling, he did as she asked. They did have plans to make—plans for a peaceful life together. But before that could happen, there was one more fight to win. In two weeks, they would meet Thelia in the Emerald City, so there was no more time to waste. He took Reva's hand in his and smiled.

"Lead the way, my love."

Epilogue

Reva

Little had changed visibly in the Emerald City. The tavern stood before Reva and Crow, the magical barrier still flickering a glittery white. All the surrounding shops needed rebuilding. The palace still held King Pastoria's barrier. Yet this time, everything was quiet after the gnomes had taken control of the capital. No fights in the streets. No battling in the air. The fae outdoors had faces filled with hope instead of despair once Crow told them Locasta and Langwidere were both dead. Soon, the Wizard would be dead too and then the palace would be Ozma's.

Reva didn't know what had happened to Ozma or when she would show up here to claim her palace. A small hint of doubt nagged inside her head—what if she didn't? But Ozma had survived so much—she would have to survive this too. Reva would give her more time, and if Ozma didn't show up, then she would have to cross the desert to find her friend.

"Are you ready?" Crow asked, interrupting her thoughts.

Reva nodded. "Yes. I'm just overthinking things."

He intertwined his fingers with hers and kissed her knuckles.

It calmed her for the moment. Giving her hand a squeeze, he pulled her through Queen Lurline's magic barrier and toward the establishment.

Two male centaurs stood outside, chatting and sipping from mugs, both fae giving them a smile as they passed. Crow opened the door, allowing Reva to enter first.

Once she stepped inside, a tangy scent hit her. Reva spotted one of the familiar dryads—Milla—talking to a young male faun with blond hair who was eating pie over a plate. She recognized the child right away.

"Birch!" Reva called, striding up to the counter. Had he gone to the South like she'd asked?

Spinning around, his gaze met hers. A grin spread across Birch's face before his lips pulled down into a frown. He poked his fork at the air. "You didn't tell me the Tin Woodsman was in the South."

Reva exchanged a glance with Crow as he came up beside her. "Would you have gone if I'd told you?"

Birch appeared deep in thought when his eyes ticked side to side. "No."

"Well, then there's your answer," she said. "How was he?"

"Eh." Birch shrugged. "He's not as bad as everyone says."

"Are you sure about that?" Crow mumbled.

"What are you saying about me?" a deep voice boomed from behind them.

Crow glanced around with a sigh. "Do you always have to lurk?"

"Only because it bothers you so much." Tin ran his gloved fingers against the iron scar on his cheek. He was dressed the same as when she'd seen him last, with kelpie scales artfully sewn into his black tunic and pants, only less bloody. An axe rested at his hip. His silver hair was pulled back in a low knot and his hungry gaze was focused on the pie in Birch's hand.

Reva's heart practically stopped when her eyes drifted from Tin to the smaller female coming up beside him. She wore a lavender dress, simple, but with stitched floral designs down the sides, and her hair in a single braid. *Thelia*. She was more beautiful than Reva remembered, and she looked more like Crow than ever.

Before Reva could move forward, Thelia threw her arms around her. "You're late meeting us here. I was worried sick."

"It took longer to set things up in the North than we'd expected." Reva smiled, letting go of her and stepping back. Not to mention that they'd had to visit Calla on the way. "With or without us, you would have been fine. You're a stronger daughter than I ever could have asked for."

"The same goes for my mother." Thelia turned to Crow next and gave him a hug before they started chatting about her meeting Whispa.

After Whispa had given Thelia instructions to meet them in the Emerald City, the pixie had returned to the Northern palace, where she was now watching over it with the other guards until Reva and Crow could return.

Since Locasta no longer reigned, the Northerners had accepted Reva despite the menacing things she'd done while cursed. It didn't hurt that she had Crow by her side, who they loved.

She'd have to work on relations in the East soon, and she hoped they would grow accustomed to her too. Apparently, Locasta had started attacking fae there with the night beasts, even though it had been her own territory. Over the years, while Reva was in the dark place, it seemed the dead witch's desire to torture had grown.

"May I talk to Thelia alone for a moment?" Reva asked.

"Of course," Crow said.

Tin didn't move.

"That means you too, dumbass." Crow shoved Tin forward. Thelia chuckled as Tin cursed under his breath. Reva watched as they went with Birch back to the counter and asked for drinks.

Reva and Thelia walked over to a table in the far corner, near the one where she'd sat the last time she was here with Crow. She pulled out a chair and took a seat across from her daughter. "How's the South been?"

"It's taking a little adjusting, but some of the fae have returned and there hasn't been any new sign of Wheelers."

"*Good.*" They were either all dead by Reva's hand when she'd killed the large group of them, or they had fled back to the outskirts of the Deadly Desert. "If Ozma doesn't meet us here in a few weeks, I may have to go searching for her." Or the Wizard.

Thelia leaned back in her seat, folding her arms. "I'm not staying back this time if you do."

"I wouldn't dare ask that of you again." Locasta would have been too dangerous and tricky for Thelia. Oz was manipulative too, but he was still mortal—silver slippers or not. "But let's hope she comes soon." Reva's gaze traveled to the counter and settled on the smaller fae. "So really, how was Birch when he first came to the palace?"

Dorothy grinned. "Tin greeted him at the door by asking who the hell he was. It took him a moment to recognize Tin before he tried to run. I had to catch Birch and persuade him to stay by giving him desserts while Tin thought I should have just let him run off."

Reva chuckled.

"I suppose we should do another story-time. How about you go first?"

"I don't think so." Thelia paused, still grinning, and shook her head. "You and Crow seem to be getting along better. I need to know more about *that.*"

Reva couldn't help focusing her attention on Crow. "Of course. I'll tell you half while my husband tells the other. We'll do it together."

"*Husband?*" Thelia's brows rose all the way up her forehead, her eyes bulging. "I knew you two would find a way back to each other, but you got *married?*"

"It happened a long time ago, actually—before we had you. Sometimes you just have to let the storm pass before the calm takes over." Reva smiled as Crow noticed her watching him from across the room. He gave her a quick wink as he took a sip from his glass and held up an apple in his other hand. "The day I met your father started with my favorite piece of fruit."

Did you enjoy Crow?

Authors always appreciate reviews, whether long or short.

Want more Faeries of Oz? Check out Ozma, Book Three, in the Faeries of Oz series!

At Ozma's birth, the witch, Mombi, abducted and cast a spell on her, turning the infant into a male. Only when Ozma broke the witch's curse did she discover who she is—the True Queen of Oz. Her freedom is short lived when the Wizard, hungry for her power, imprisons her in a dark, brutal world, cut off from Jack and her magic.

Jack, too, was stolen as a child, forced to toil as Mombi's slave. When he believed his lover died, Jack loses himself to an array of companions, while plotting his escape from Mombi.

Once Ozma is returned to the Land of Oz by a savior's magic, she seeks to reunite with Jack while vowing to kill the two fae who ruined their lives. However, neither Jack or Ozma are the same as they once were. They must put their heartache aside to journey across the unforgiving land to stop the Wizard and keep evil from sweeping over the territories.

Acknowledgments

For all the readers that have continued with this series, thank you so incredibly much! We hope you loved reading our version of Oz as much as we've enjoyed writing it!

To our families and friends, you are what gives us this ongoing writing inspiration. We'd like to give big hugs to Elle, Tracy, Donna, Amber H., Jenny, Lauren, Lindsay, Loretta, and Victoria for helping us once again.

Crow and Reva had so much emotion that was yearning to break through! And we'll tell you now, Ozma and Jack's love is going to be the most emotional of all!

About the Authors

Amber R. Duell was born and raised in a small town in Central New York. While it will always be home, she's constantly moving with her husband and two sons as a military wife. She does her best writing in the middle of the night, surviving the daylight hours with massive amounts of caffeine. When not reading or writing, she enjoys snowboarding, embroidering, and snuggling with her cats.

Candace Robinson spends her days consumed by words and hoping to one day find her own DeLorean time machine. Her life consists of avoiding migraines, admiring Bonsai trees, watching classic movies, and living with her husband and daughter in Texas—where it can be forty degrees one day and eighty the next.

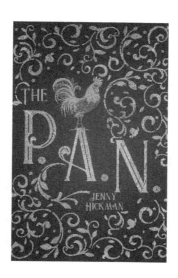

The PAN by Jenny Hickman

Since her parents were killed, Vivienne has always felt
ungrounded, shuffled through the foster care system. Just when
liberation finally seems possible—days before her eighteenth
birthday—Vivienne is hospitalized with symptoms no one can
explain.

The doctors may be puzzled, but Deacon, her mysterious new
friend, claims she has an active Nevergene. His far-fetched
diagnosis comes with a warning: she is about to become an
involuntary test subject for Humanitarian Organization for
Order and Knowledge—or HOOK. Vivienne can either escape
to Neverland's Kensington Academy and learn to fly (Did he
really just say fly?) or risk sticking around to become a human
lab rat. But accepting a place among The PAN means Vivienne
must abandon her life and foster family to safeguard their
secrets and hide in Neverland's shadows… forever.

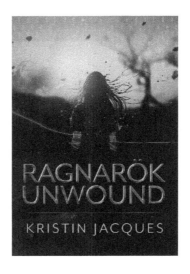

Ragnarök Unwound by Kristin Jacques

Prophecies don't untangle themselves.

Just ask Ikepela Ives, whose estranged mother left her with the power to unravel the binding threads of fate. Stuck with immortal power in a mortal body, Ives has turned her back on the duty she never wanted.

But it turns out she can't run from her fate forever, not now that Ragnarok has been set in motion and the god at the center of that tangled mess has gone missing. With a ragtag group of companions—including a brownie, a Valkyrie, and the goddess of death herself—Ives embarks on her first official mission as Fate Cipher—to save the world from doomsday.

Nothing she can't handle. Right?

CPSIA information can be obtained
at www.ICGtesting.com
Printed in the USA
LVHW030805290121
677755LV00006B/1368